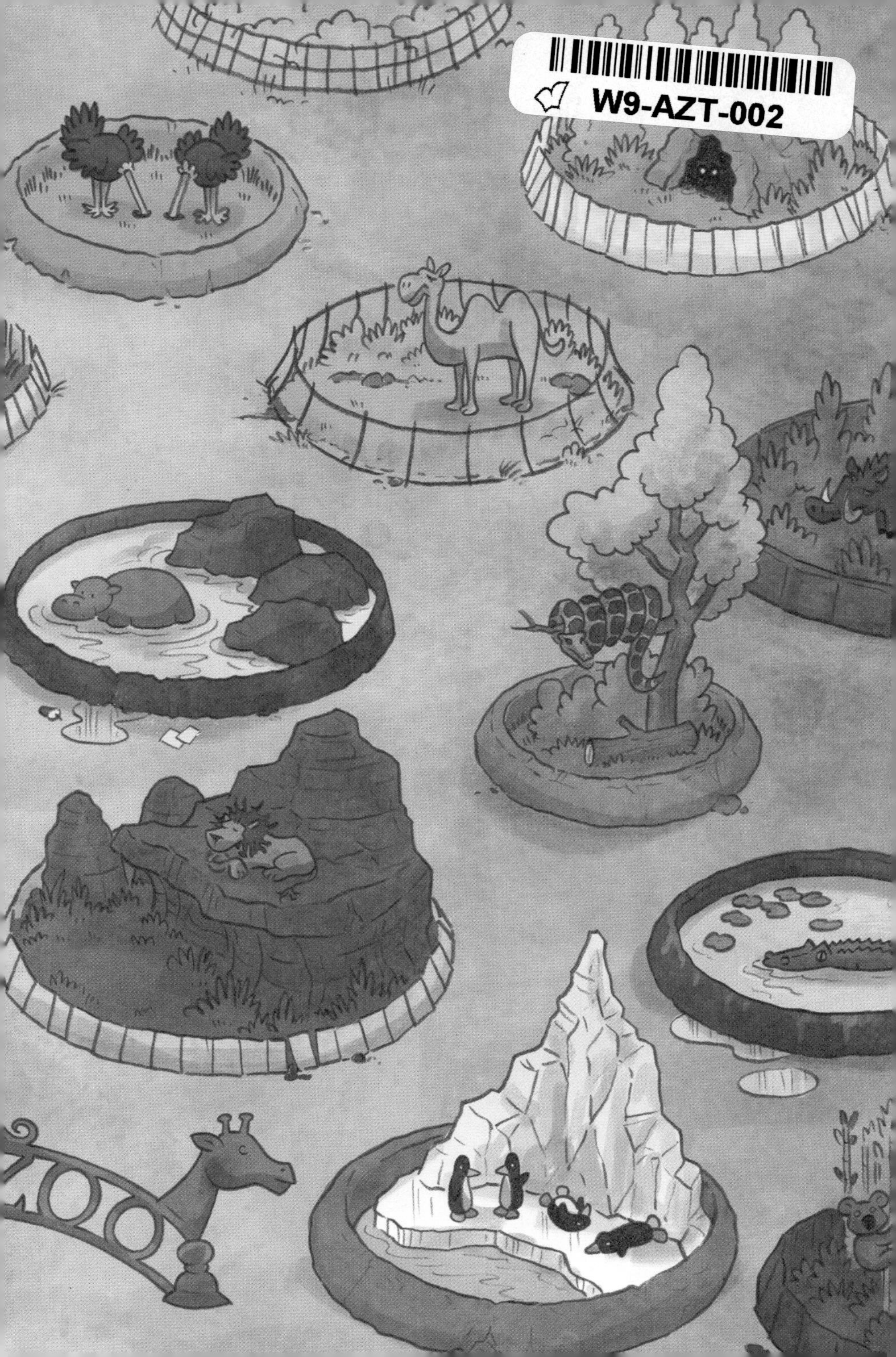
ZOO

HIPPOPOTAMISTER

HIPPOPOTAMISTER

john patrick green

with color by cat caro

:01

First Second
New York

Special thanks—
to my family; to Calista Brill, Gina Gagliano, Danielle Ceccolini, Mark Siegel, and Colleen AF Venable; to Cat for her amazing colors; to Dave Roman, Raina Telgemeier, Jerzy Drozd, Zack Giallongo, and all my friends in comics; to *Geek Mom*, *Mr. Schu Reads*, *The Beat*, *SLJ Good Comics for Kids*, *Geek Dad*, *Seven Impossible Things Before Breakfast*, and *Nerdy Book Club*; to librarians, teachers, and booksellers; and to adorable animals everywhere.

:01

First Second

Copyright © 2016 by John Patrick Green
All rights reserved.

Hippopotamister was drawn on Strathmore Bristol vellum with Staedtler 2B, 3B, and 6B pencils, and digitally colored in Photoshop.

Published by First Second
First Second is an imprint of Roaring Brook Press,
a division of Holtzbrinck Publishing Holdings Limited Partnership
120 Broadway, New York, NY 10271
firstsecondbooks.com
mackids.com

Cataloging-in-Publication Data is on file at the Library of Congress
ISBN 978-1-62672-200-2

Our books may be purchased in bulk for promotional, educational, or business use.
Please contact your local bookseller or the Macmillan Corporate and Premium
Sales Department at (800) 221-7945 ext. 5442 or by email at
MacmillanSpecialSales@macmillan.com.

First edition, 2016
Revised edition, 2021
Book design by Danielle Ceccolini and John Green
Printed in China by Toppan Leefung Printing Ltd., Dongguan City, Guangdong Province

1 3 5 7 9 10 8 6 4 2

BY ART
WE LIVE

To my favorite thing

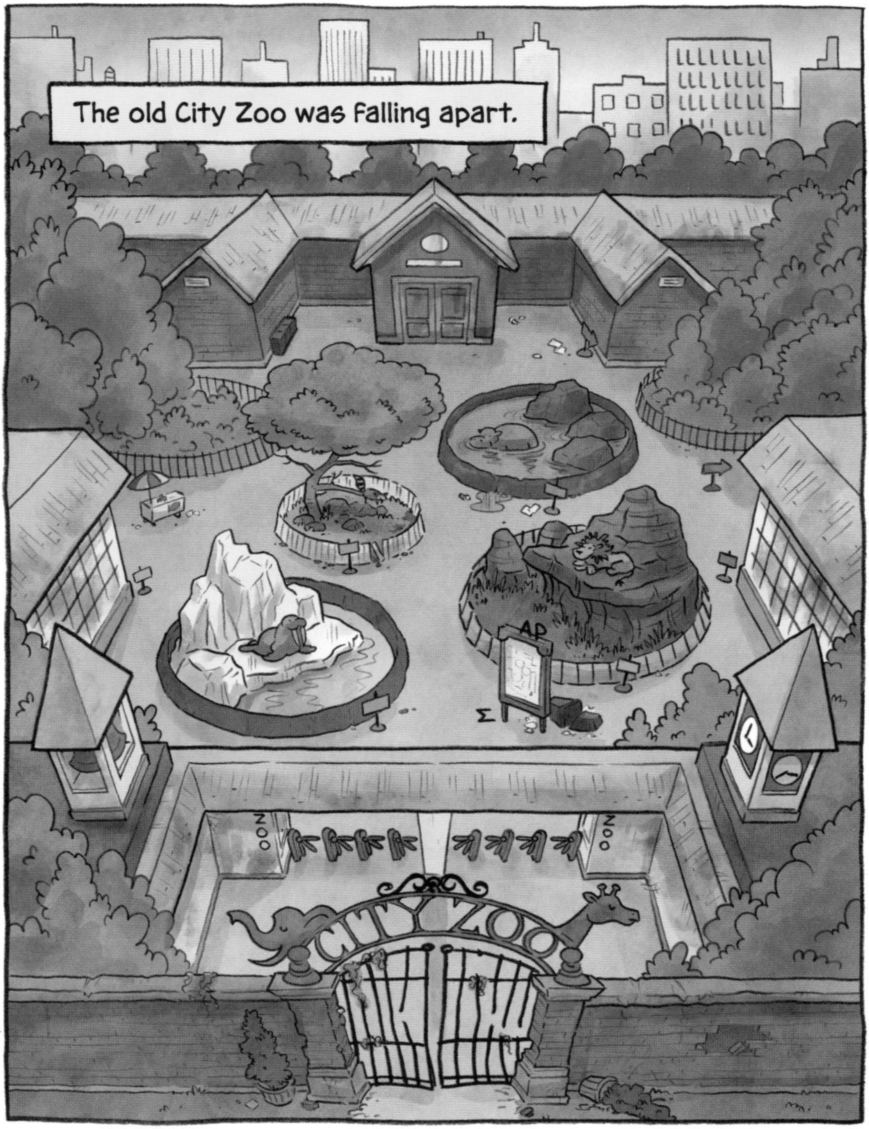
The old City Zoo was falling apart.
CITY ZOO

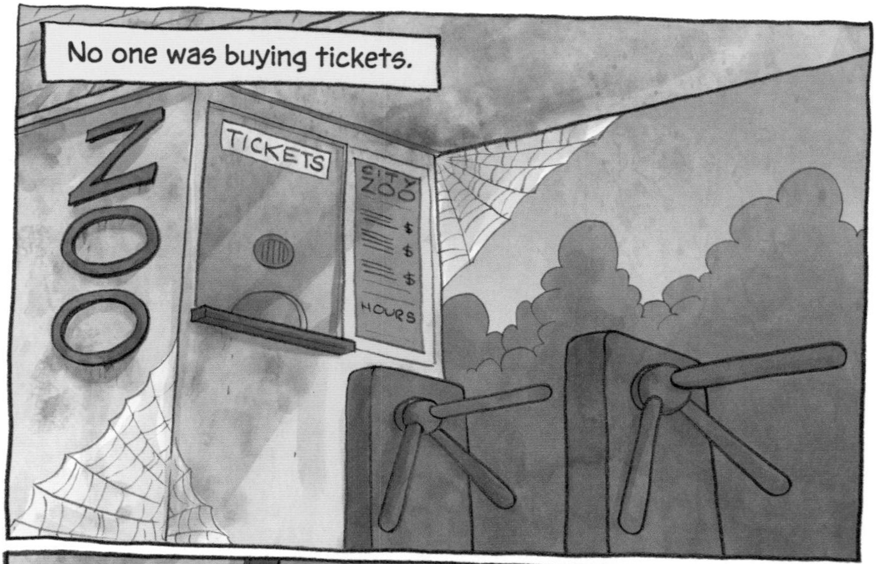
No one was buying tickets.
ZOO
TICKETS
CITY ZOO
$
$
$
HOURS

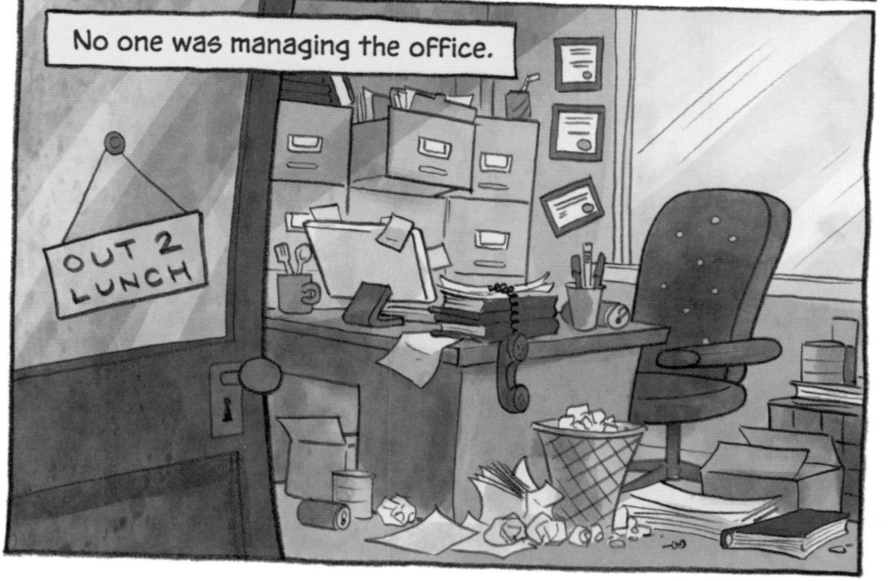
No one was managing the office.
OUT 2 LUNCH

The habitats needed repair.

TO THE EGRETS

The monkeys had no energy.

The lion's mane wasn't very regal.

The walrus's smile wasn't very bright.

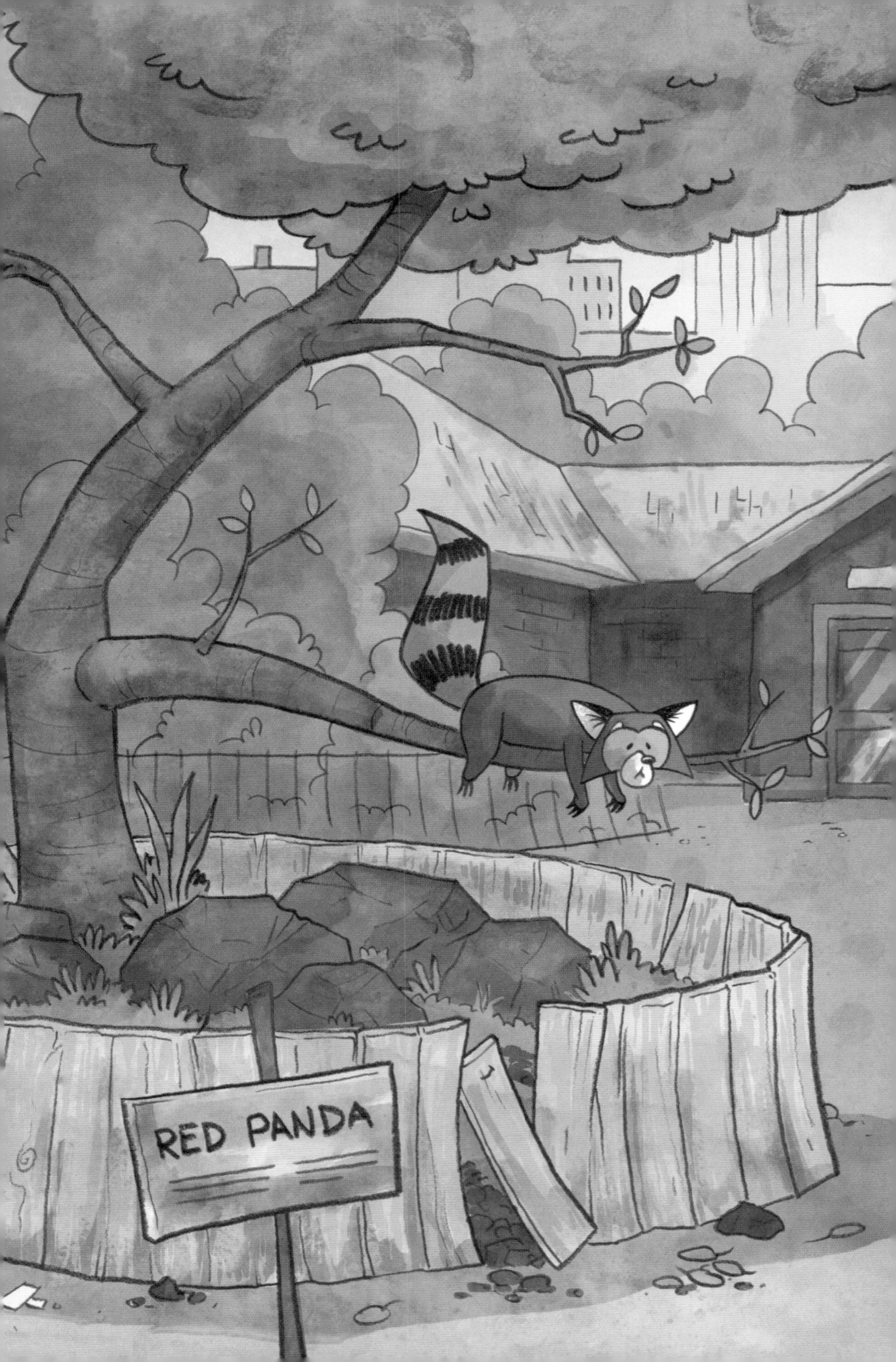
RED PANDA

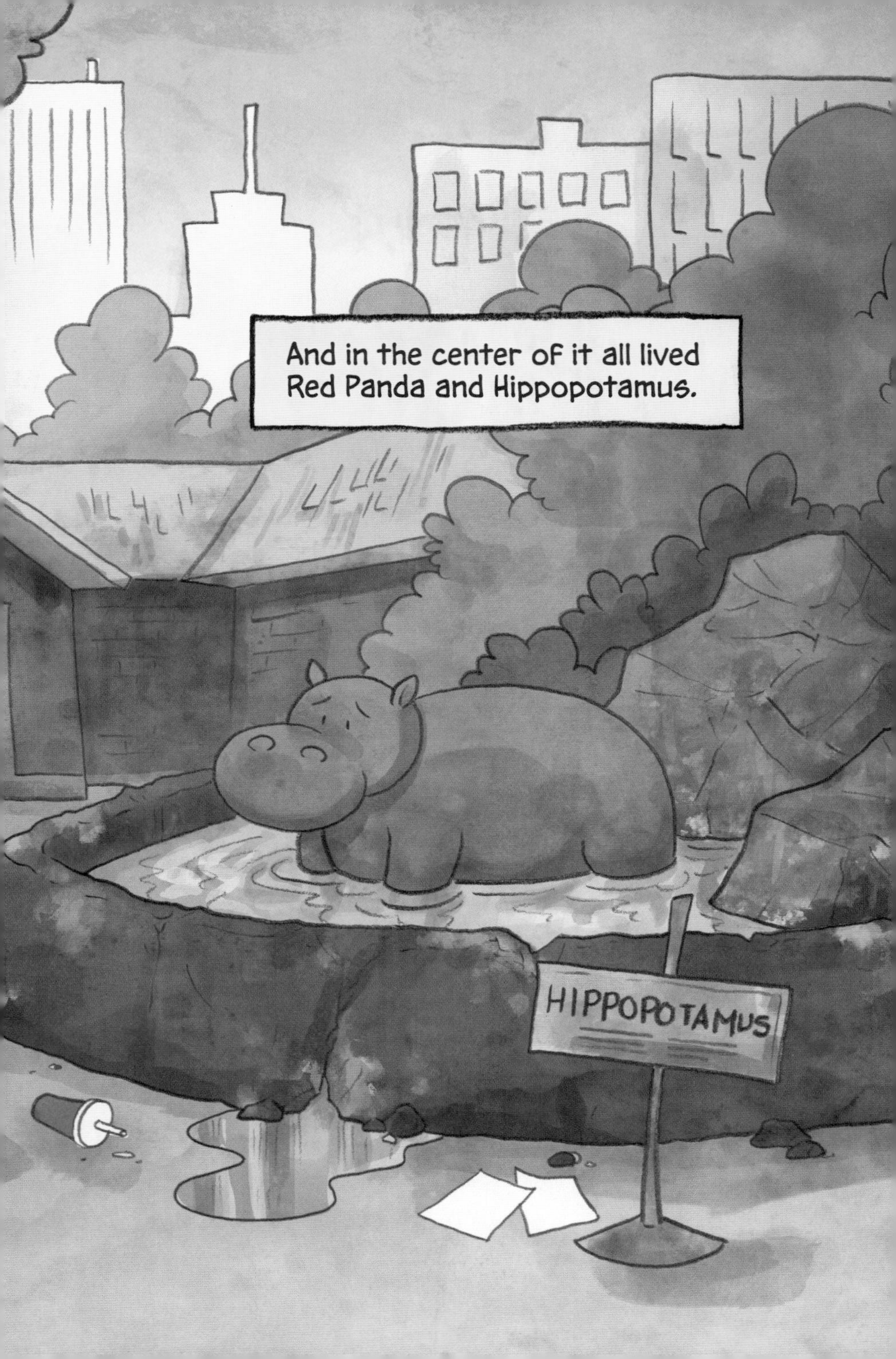
And in the center of it all lived
Red Panda and Hippopotamus.
HIPPOPOTAMUS

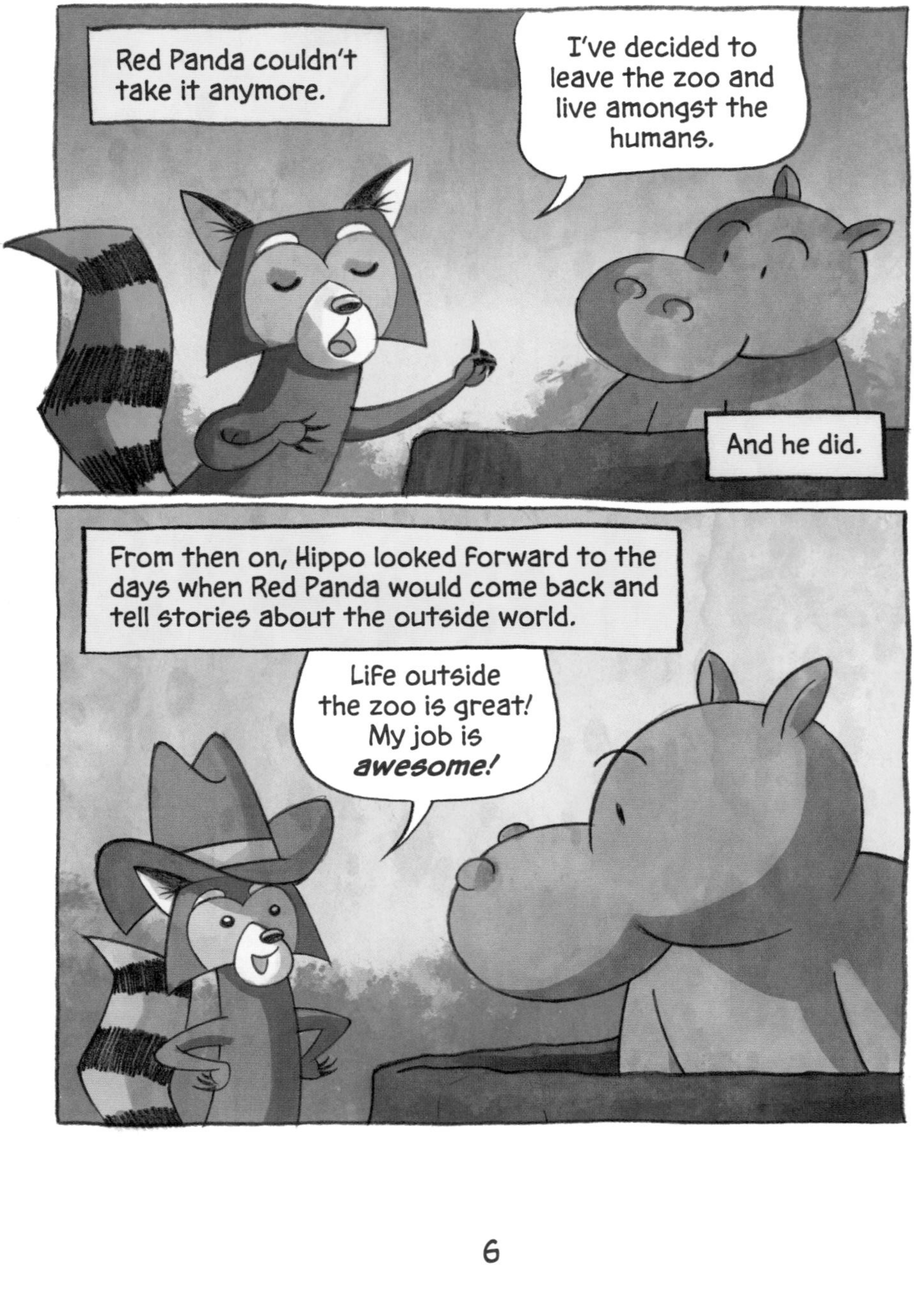
Red Panda couldn't take it anymore.
I've decided to leave the zoo and live amongst the humans.
And he did.
From then on, Hippo looked forward to the days when Red Panda would come back and tell stories about the outside world.
Life outside the zoo is great! My job is ***awesome!***

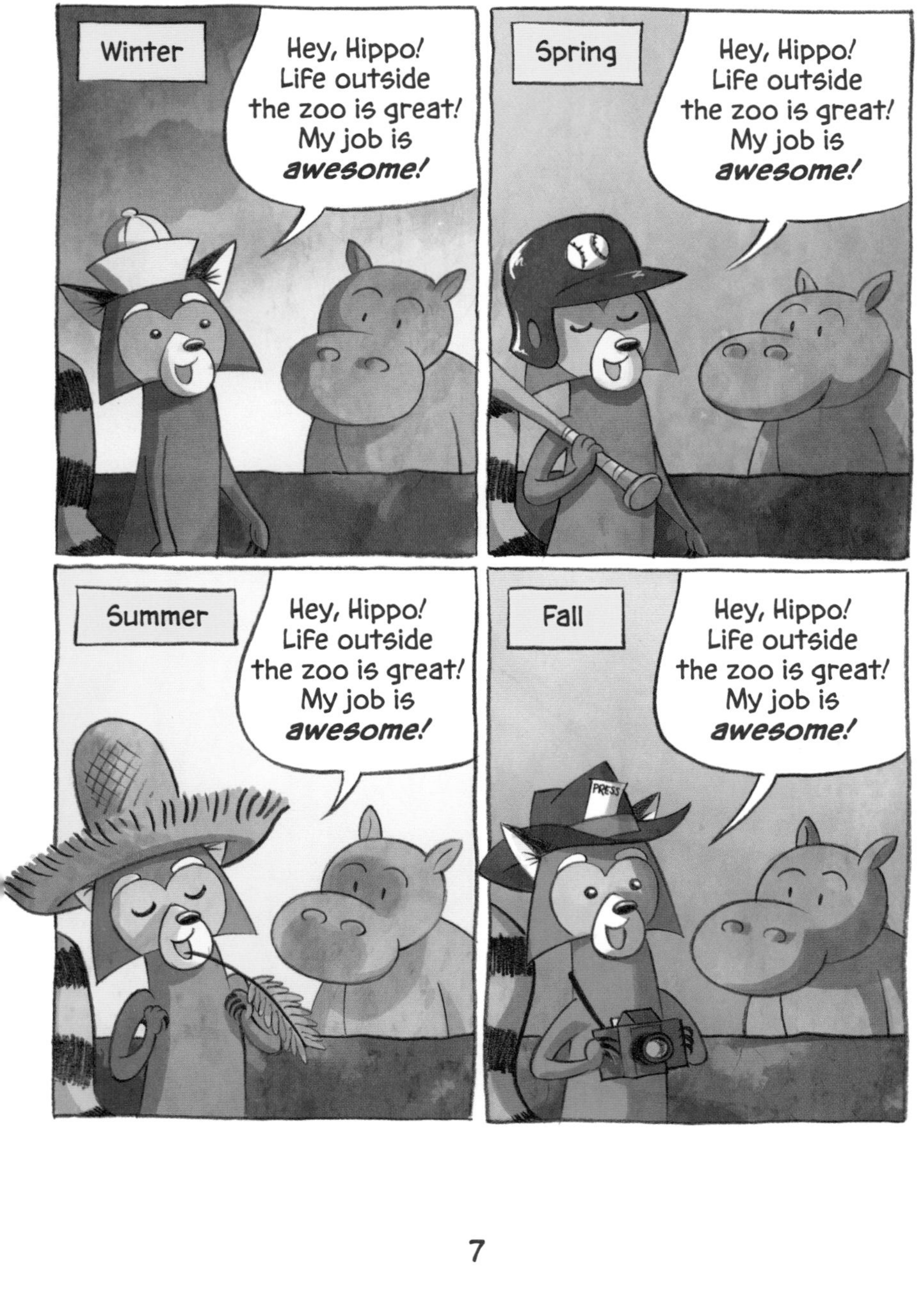
Winter
Hey, Hippo! Life outside the zoo is great! My job is ***awesome!***
Spring
Hey, Hippo! Life outside the zoo is great! My job is ***awesome!***
Summer
Hey, Hippo! Life outside the zoo is great! My job is ***awesome!***
Fall
Hey, Hippo! Life outside the zoo is great! My job is ***awesome!***
PRESS

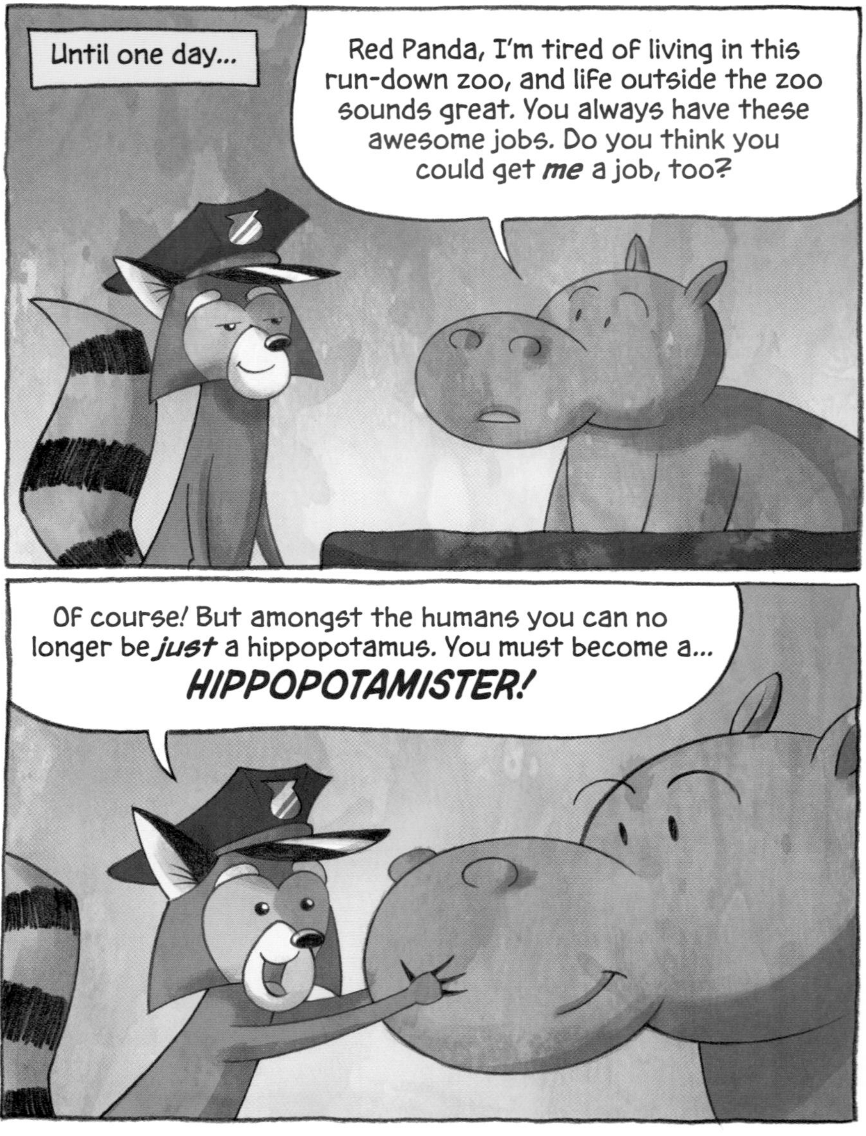
Until one day...
Red Panda, I'm tired of living in this run-down zoo, and life outside the zoo sounds great. You always have these awesome jobs. Do you think you could get *me* a job, too?
Of course! But amongst the humans you can no longer be *just* a hippopotamus. You must become a... ***HIPPOPOTAMISTER!***

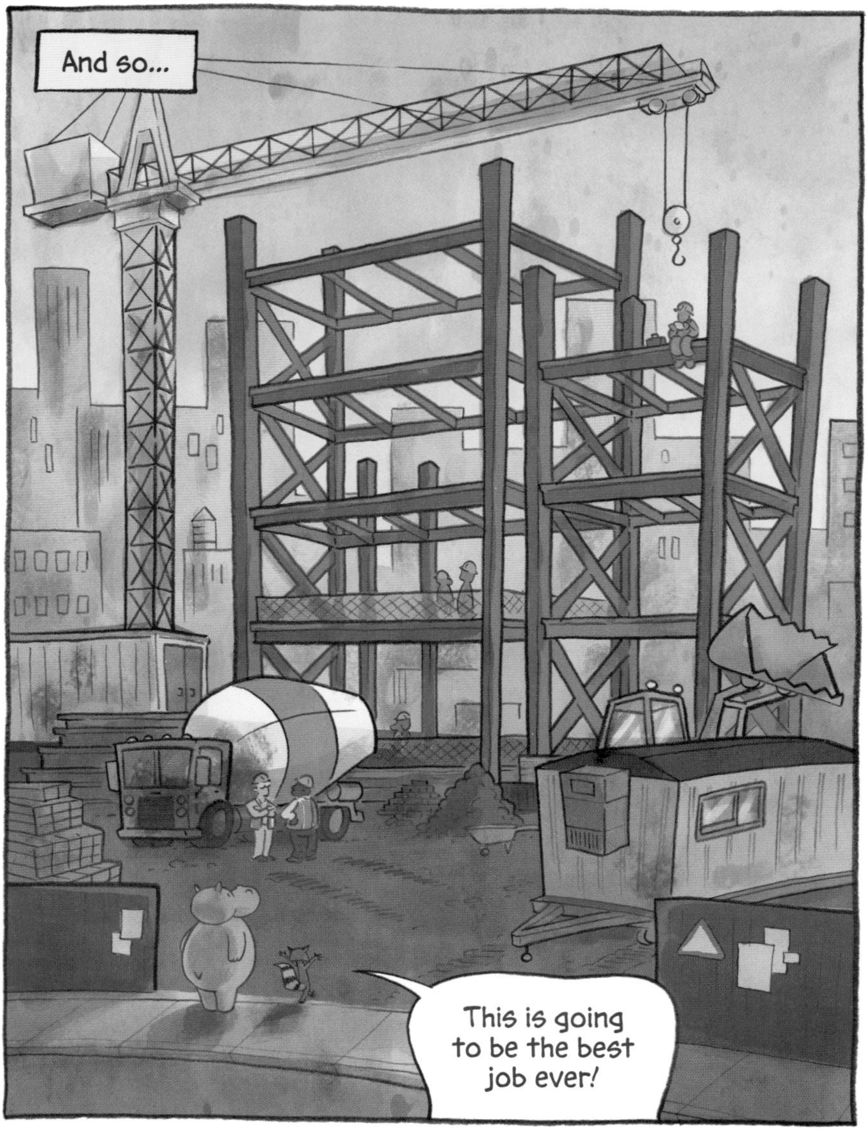
And so...
This is going to be the best job ever!

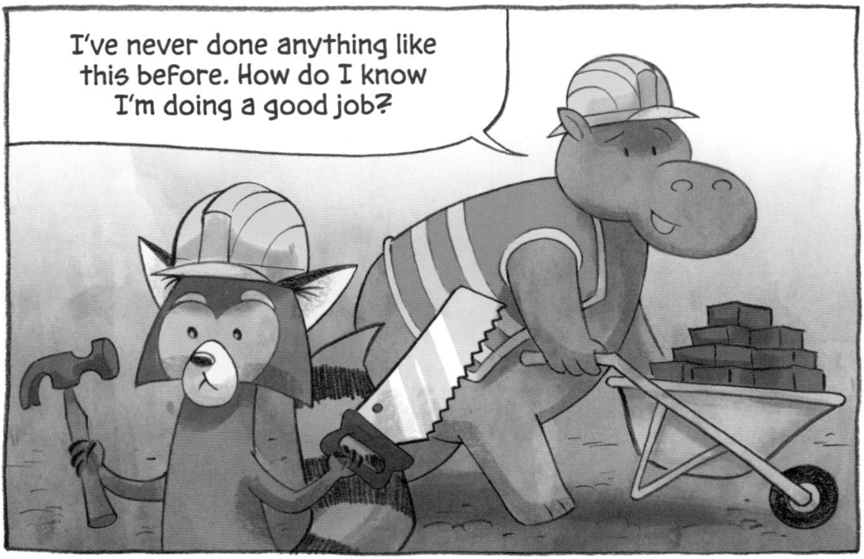
I've never done anything like this before. How do I know I'm doing a good job?

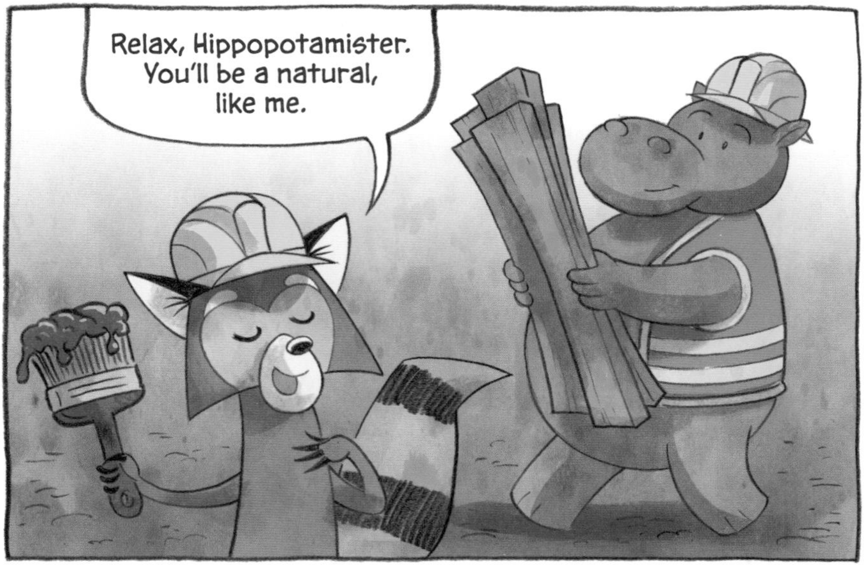
Relax, Hippopotamister. You'll be a natural, like me.

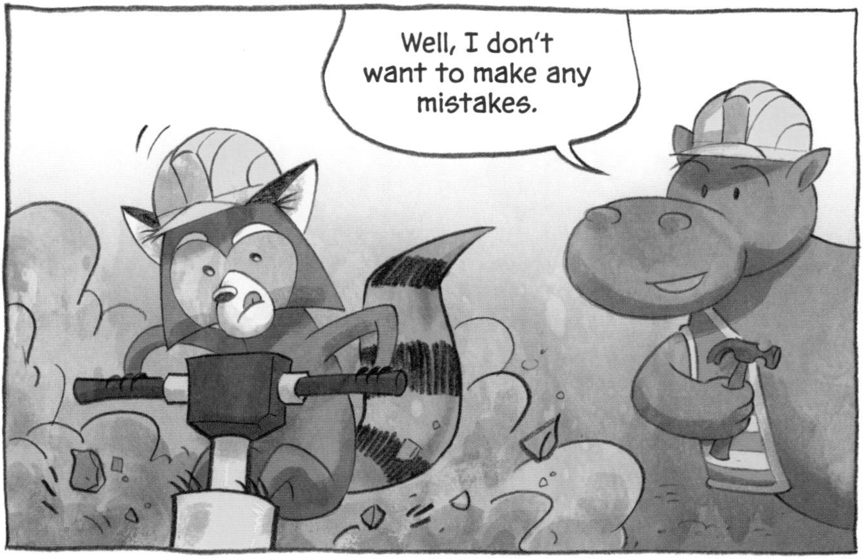
Well, I don't want to make any mistakes.

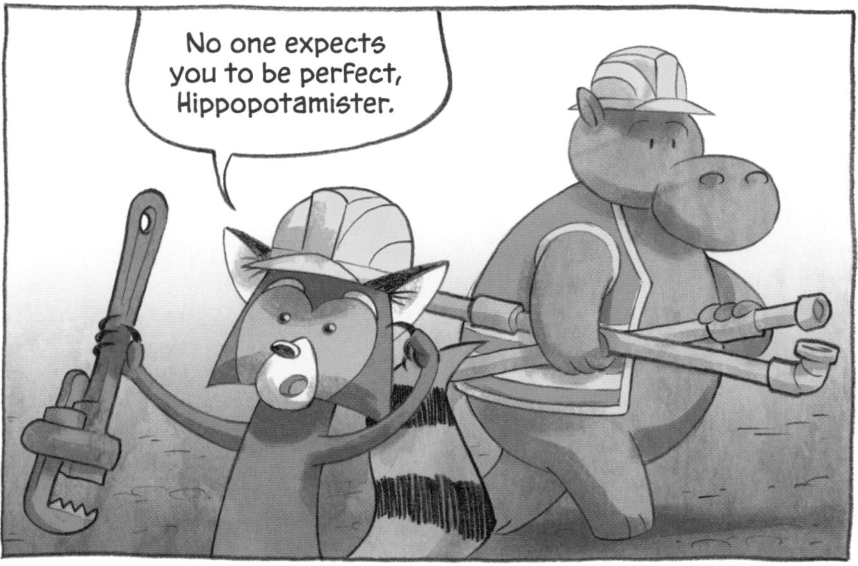
No one expects you to be perfect, Hippopotamister.

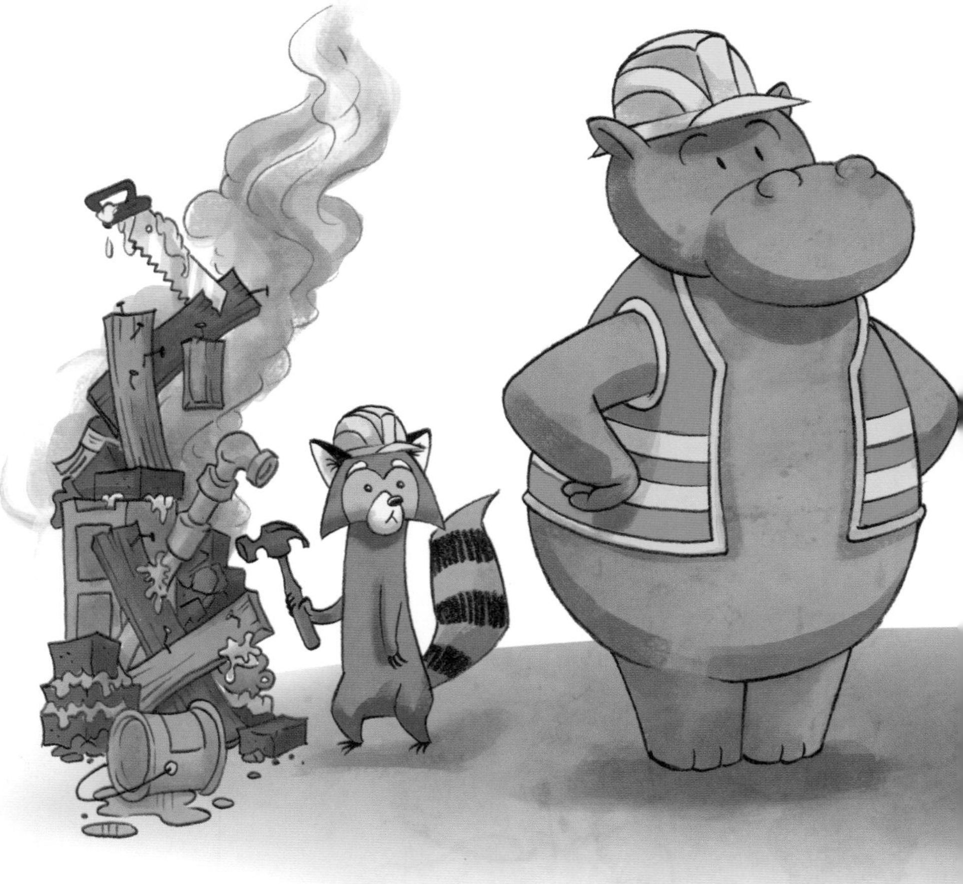

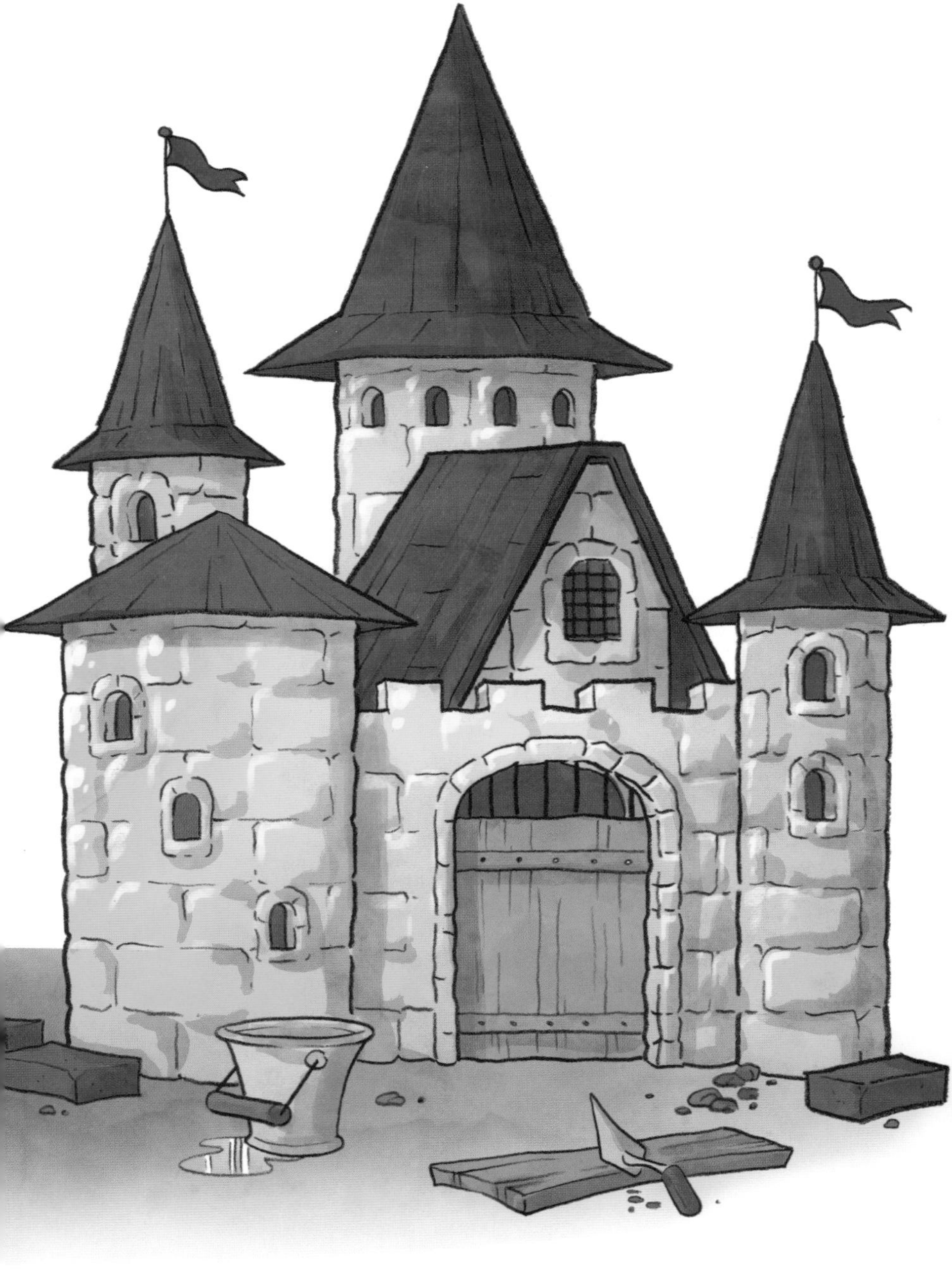

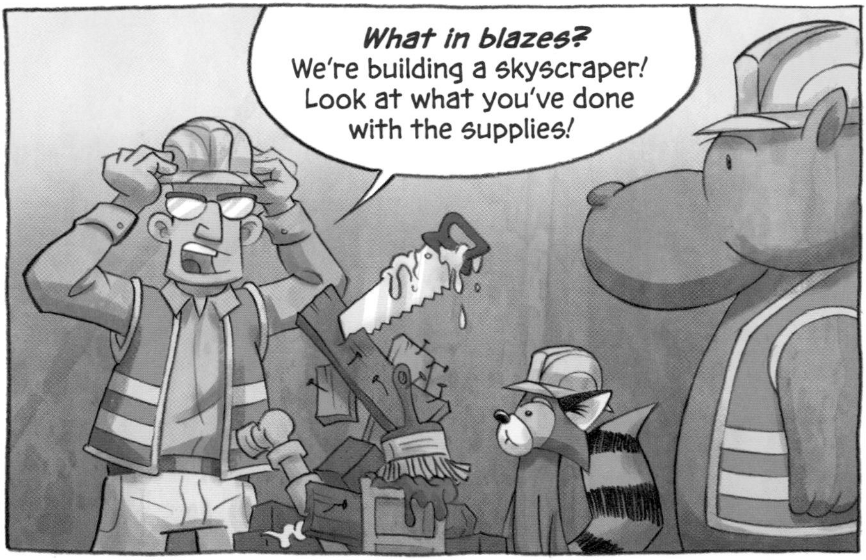
What in blazes? We're building a skyscraper! Look at what you've done with the supplies!

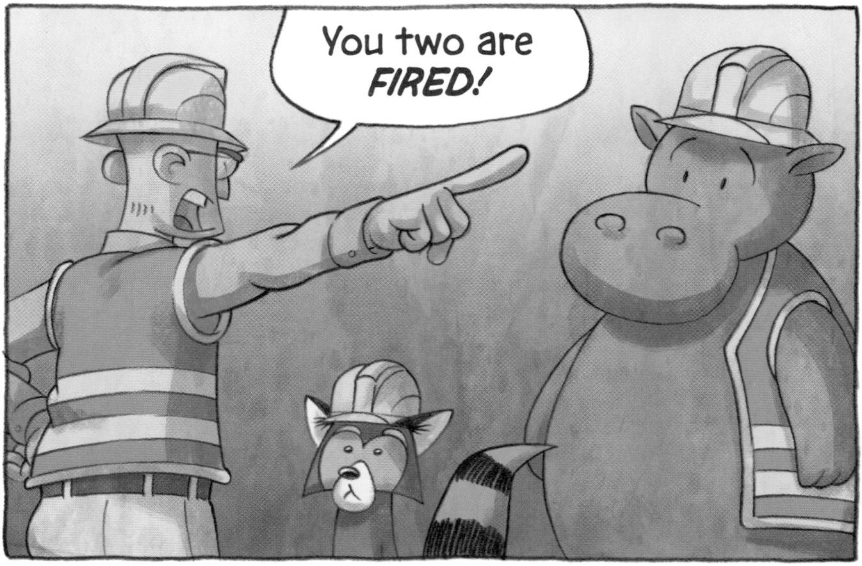
You two are FIRED!

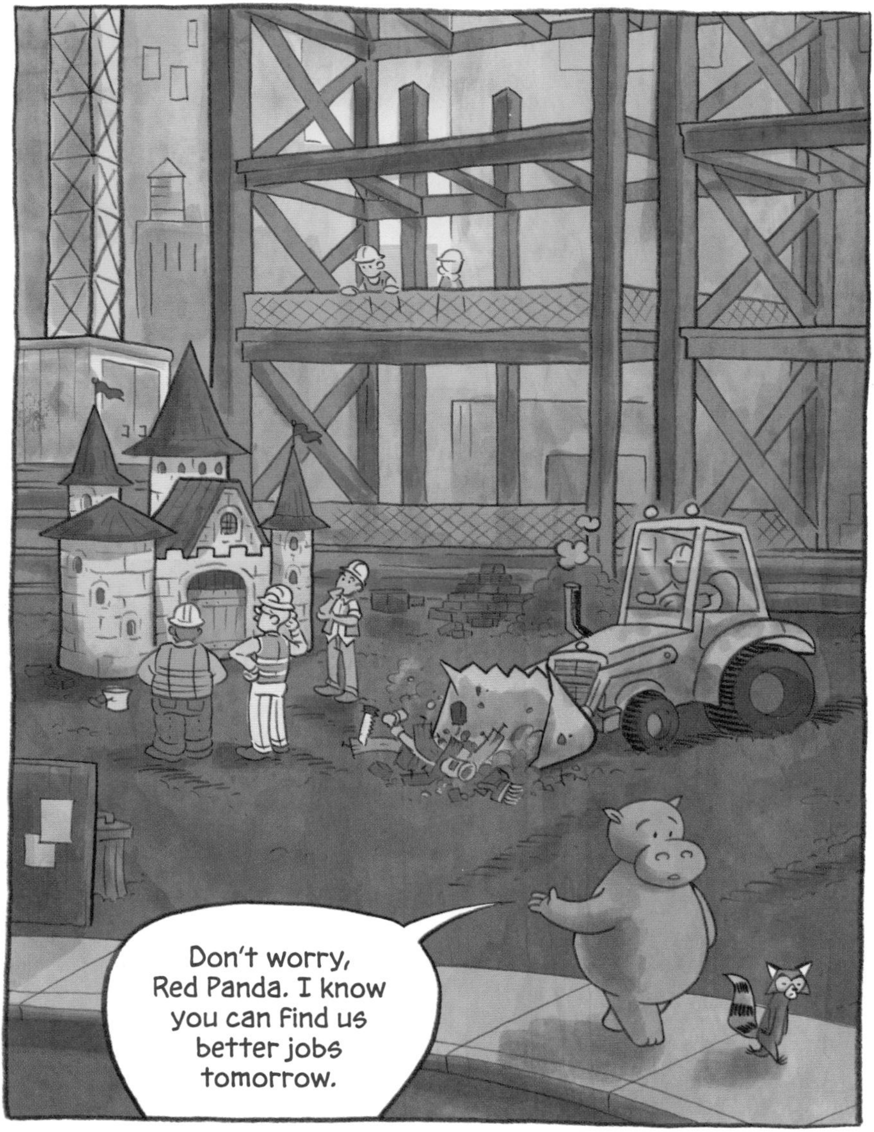
Don't worry, Red Panda. I know you can find us better jobs tomorrow.

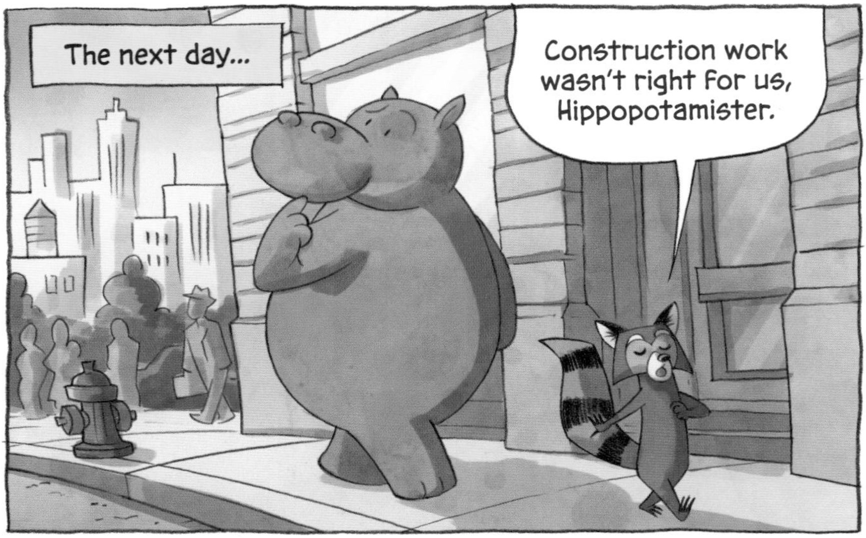
The next day...
Construction work wasn't right for us, Hippopotamister.

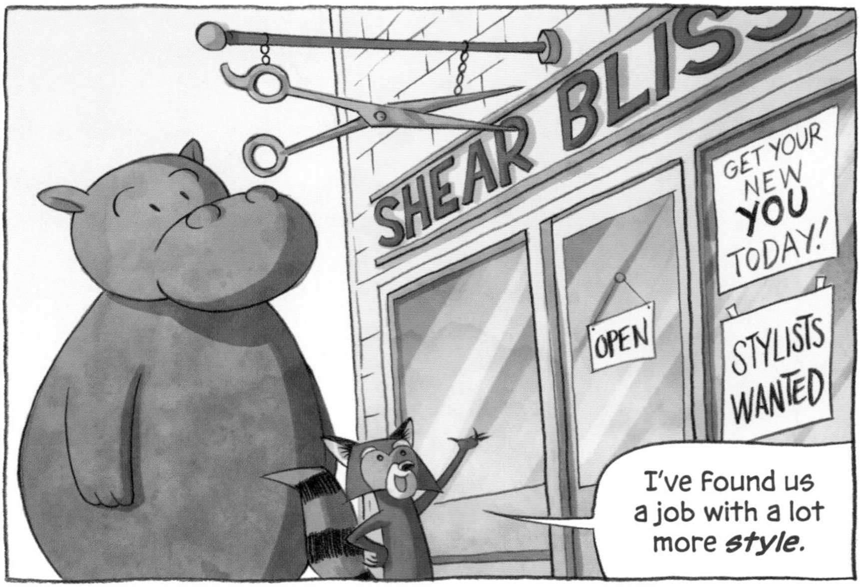
SHEAR BLISS
GET YOUR NEW YOU TODAY!
OPEN
STYLISTS WANTED
I've found us a job with a lot more *style*.

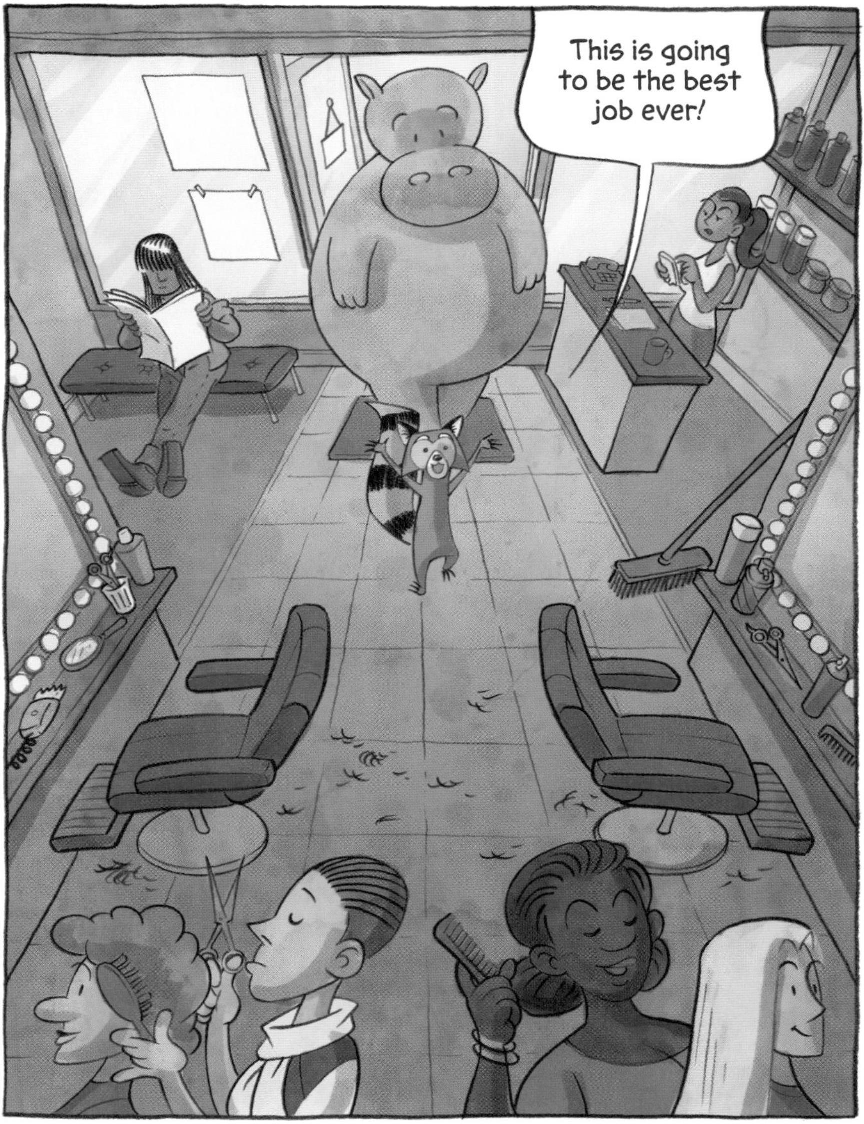
This is going to be the best job ever!

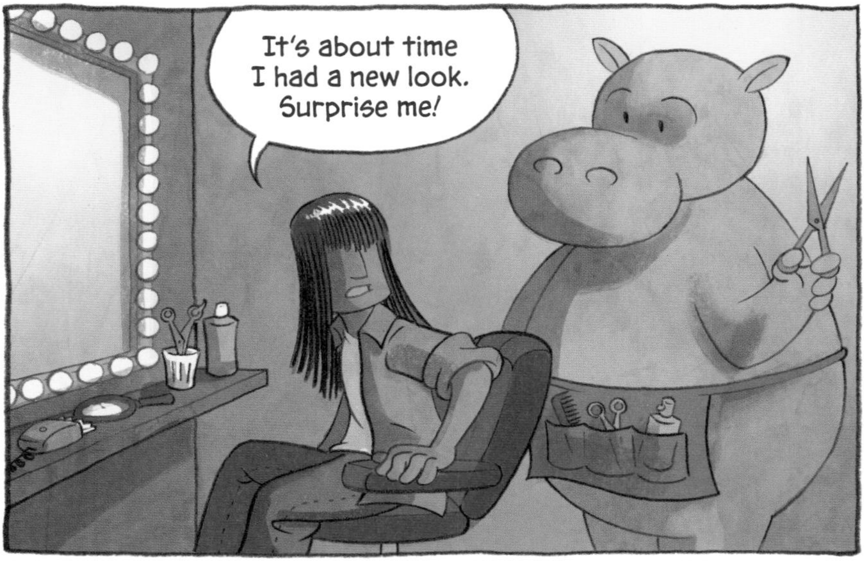
It's about time I had a new look. Surprise me!

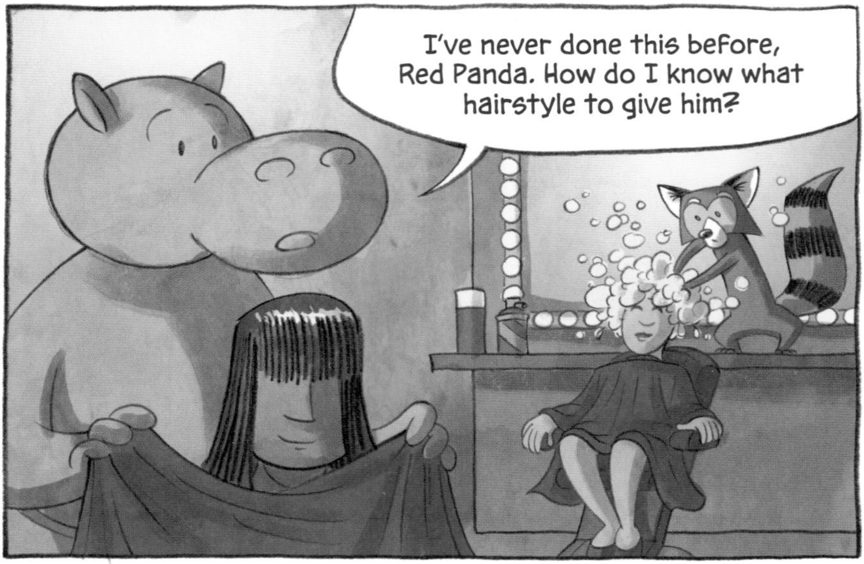
I've never done this before, Red Panda. How do I know what hairstyle to give him?

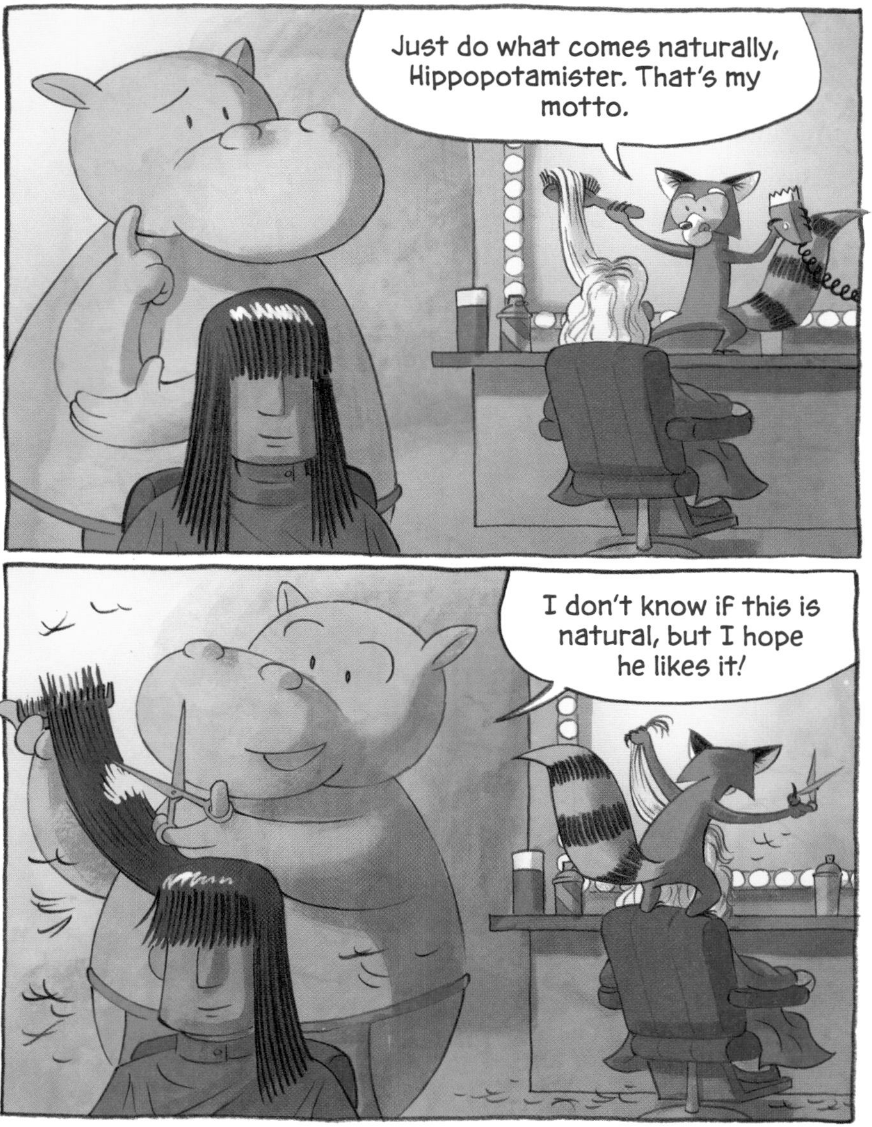
Just do what comes naturally, Hippopotamister. That's my motto.
I don't know if this is natural, but I hope he likes it!

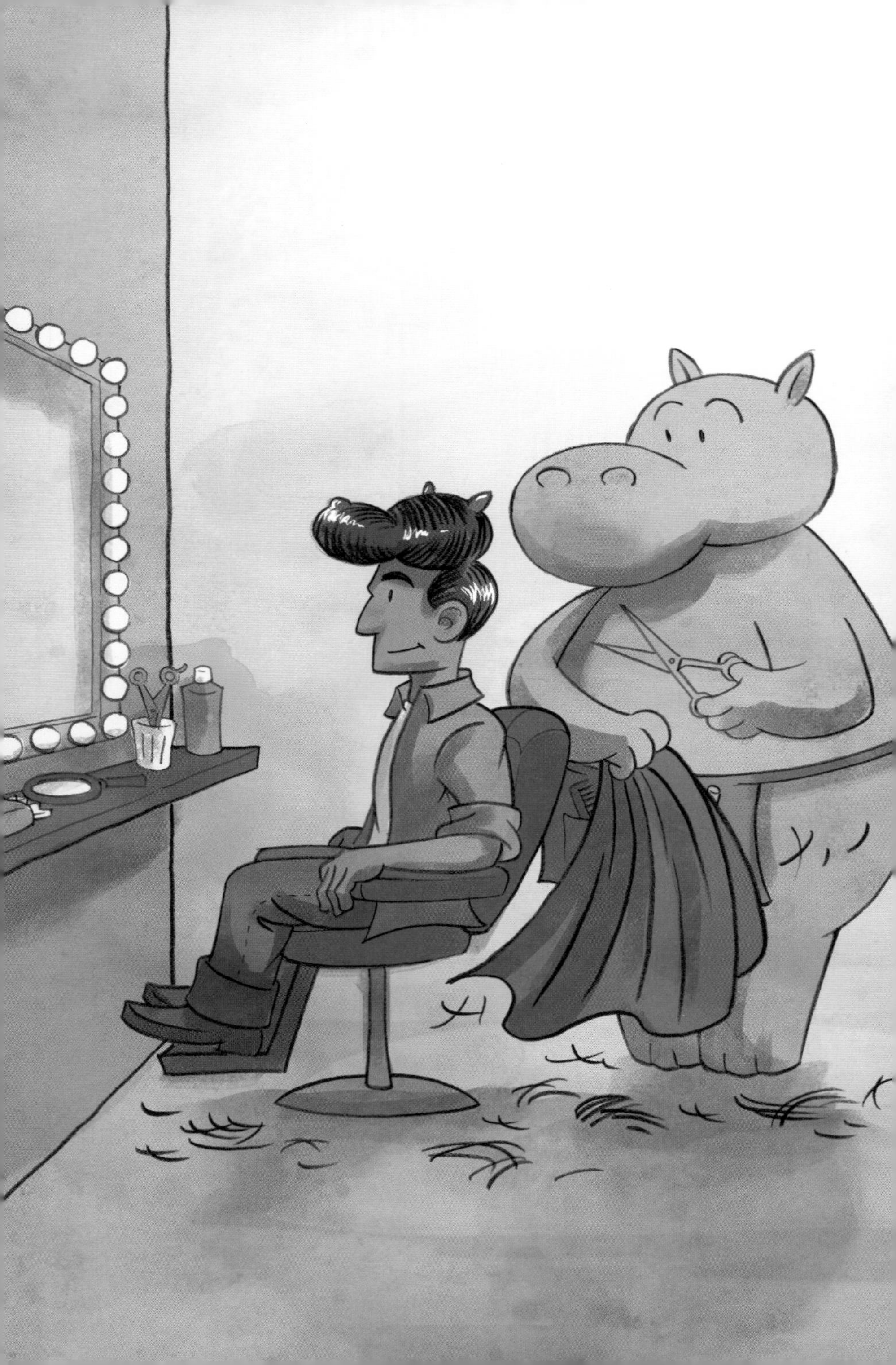

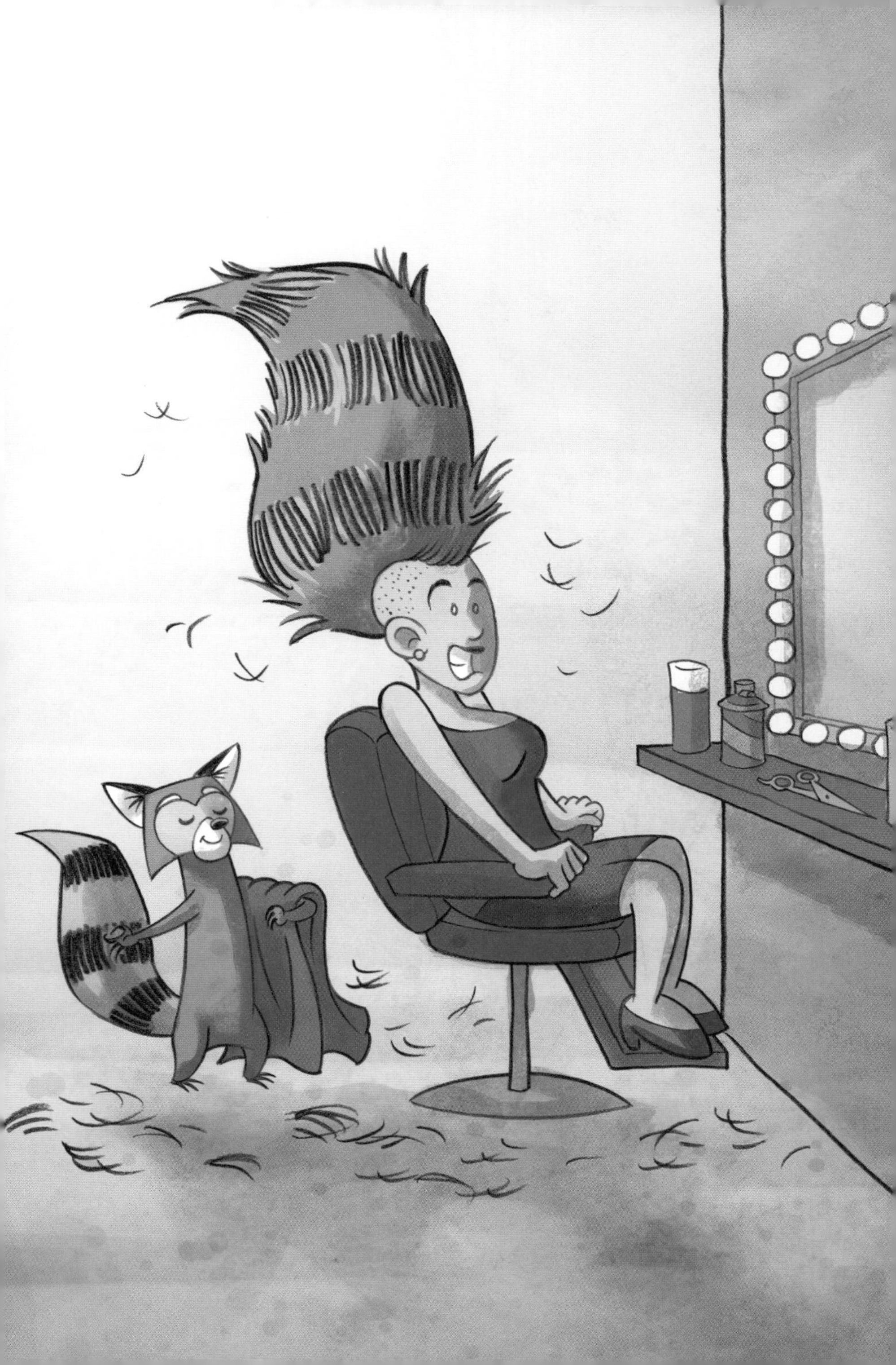

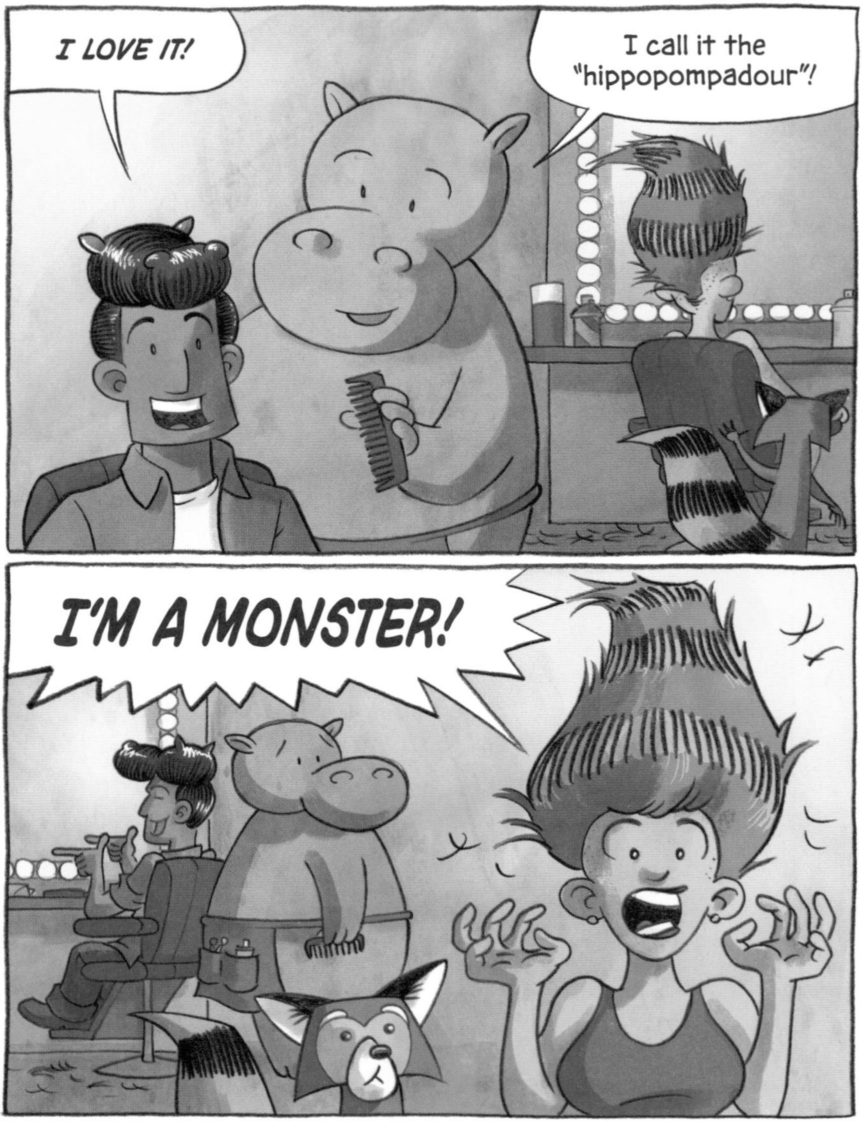
I LOVE IT!
I call it the "hippopompadour"!
I'M A MONSTER!

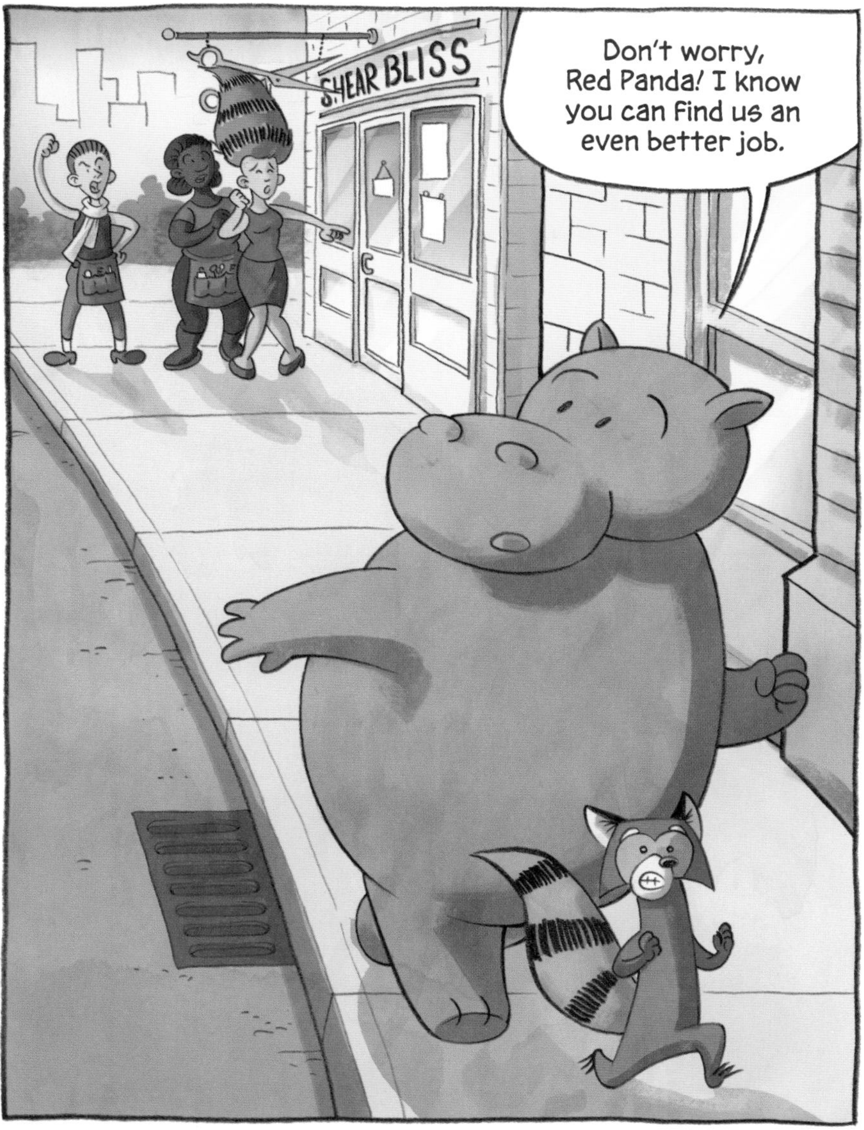
SHEAR BLISS
Don't worry, Red Panda! I know you can find us an even better job.

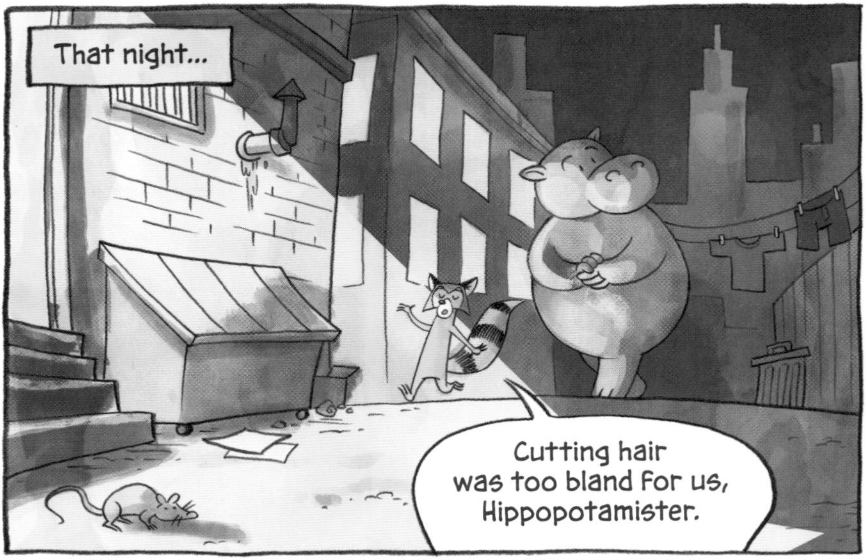
That night...
Cutting hair was too bland for us, Hippopotamister.

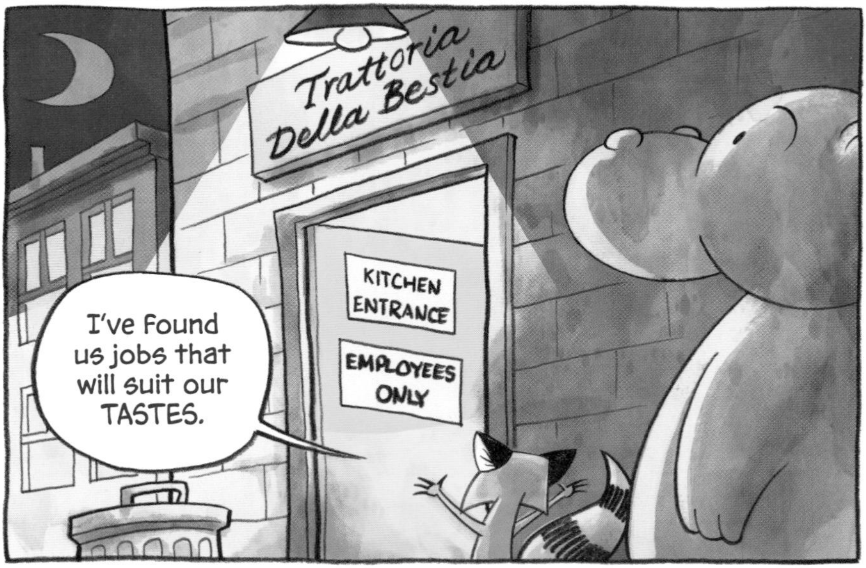
Trattoria Della Bestia
KITCHEN ENTRANCE
EMPLOYEES ONLY
I've found us jobs that will suit our TASTES.

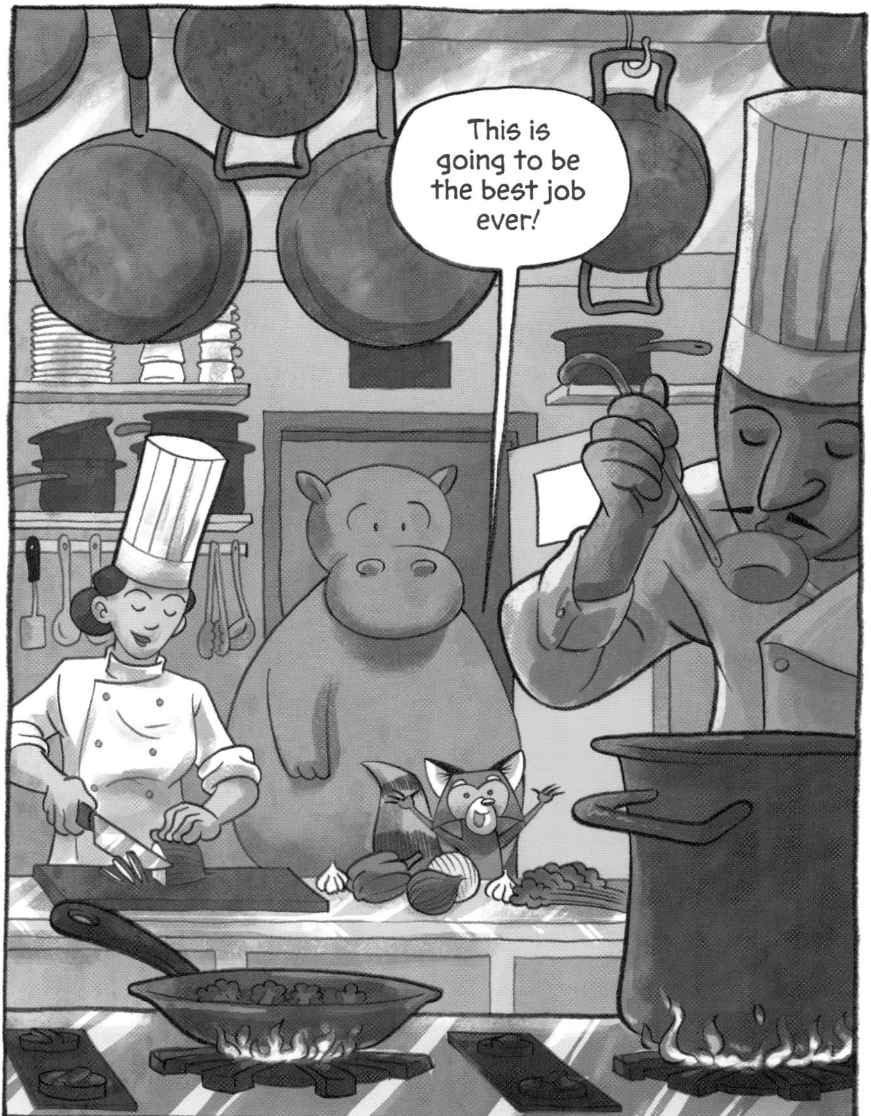
This is going to be the best job ever!

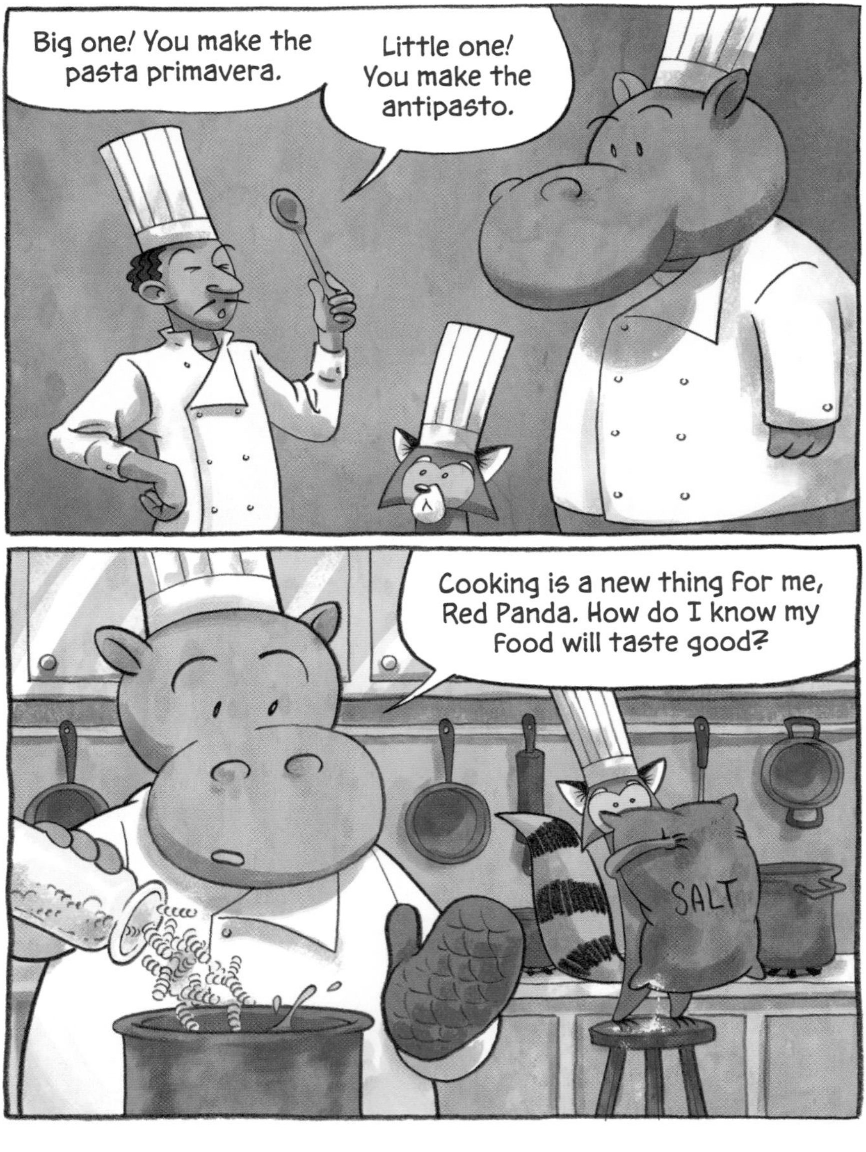
Big one! You make the pasta primavera.
Little one! You make the antipasto.
Cooking is a new thing for me, Red Panda. How do I know my food will taste good?
SALT

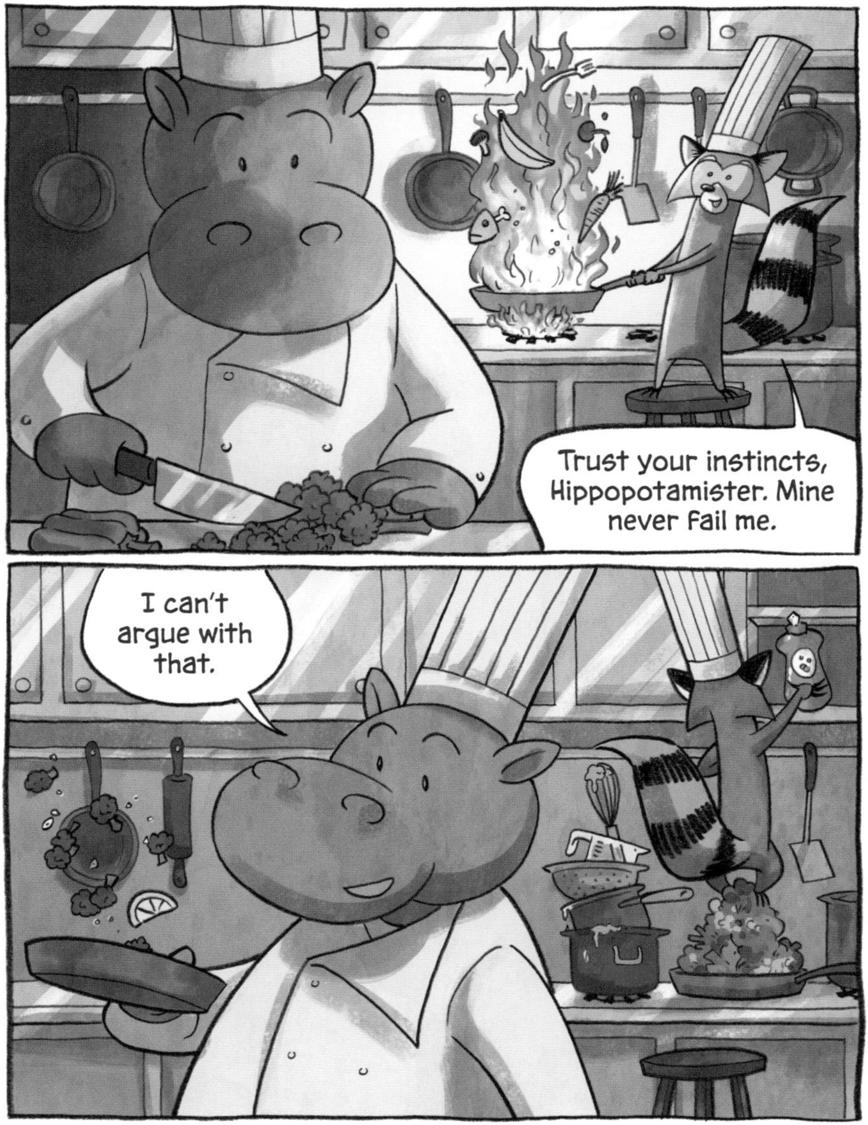
Trust your instincts, Hippopotamister. Mine never fail me.
I can't argue with that.

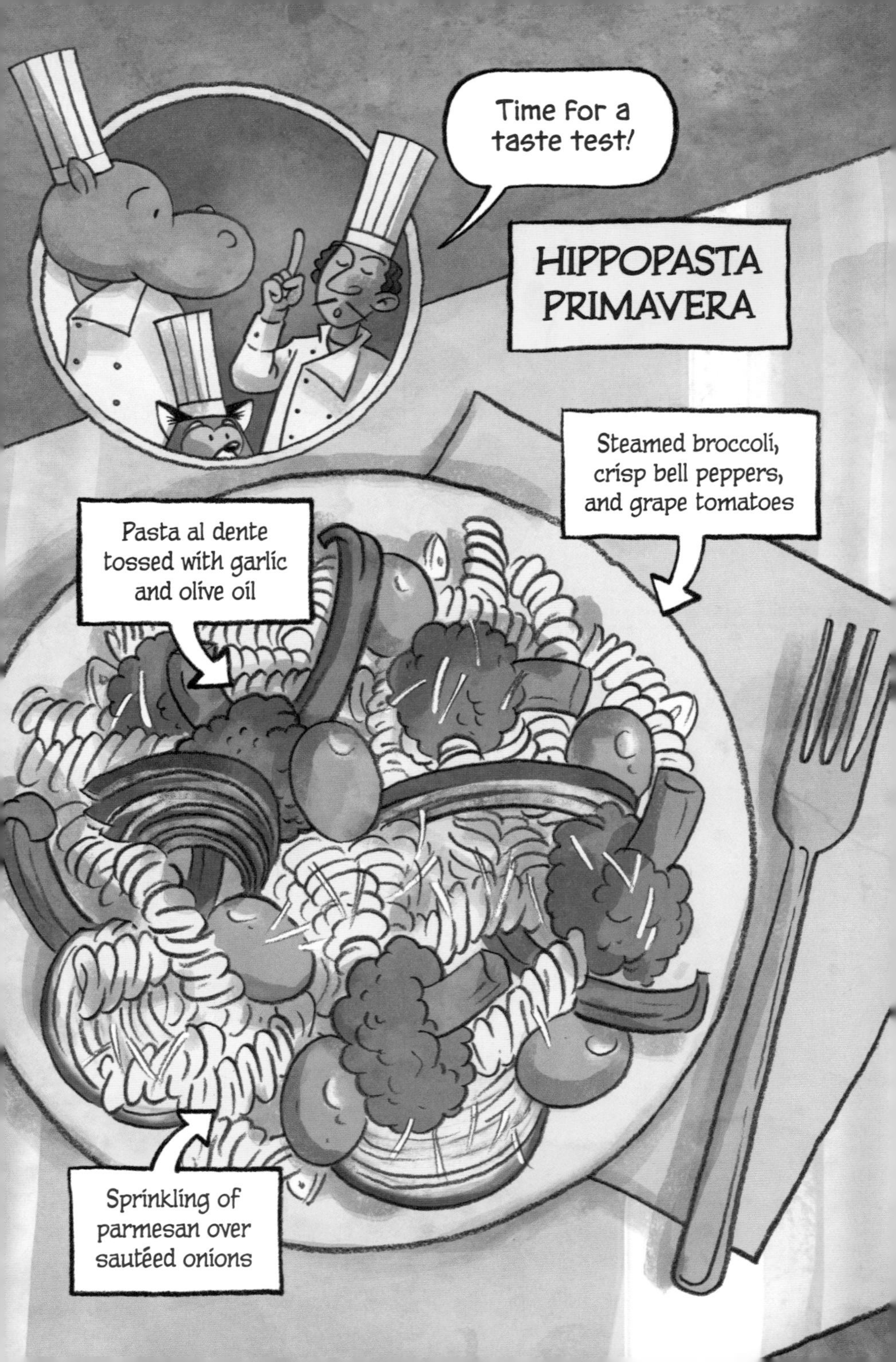

Time for a taste test!
HIPPOPASTA PRIMAVERA
Steamed broccoli, crisp bell peppers, and grape tomatoes
Pasta al dente tossed with garlic and olive oil
Sprinkling of parmesan over sautéed onions

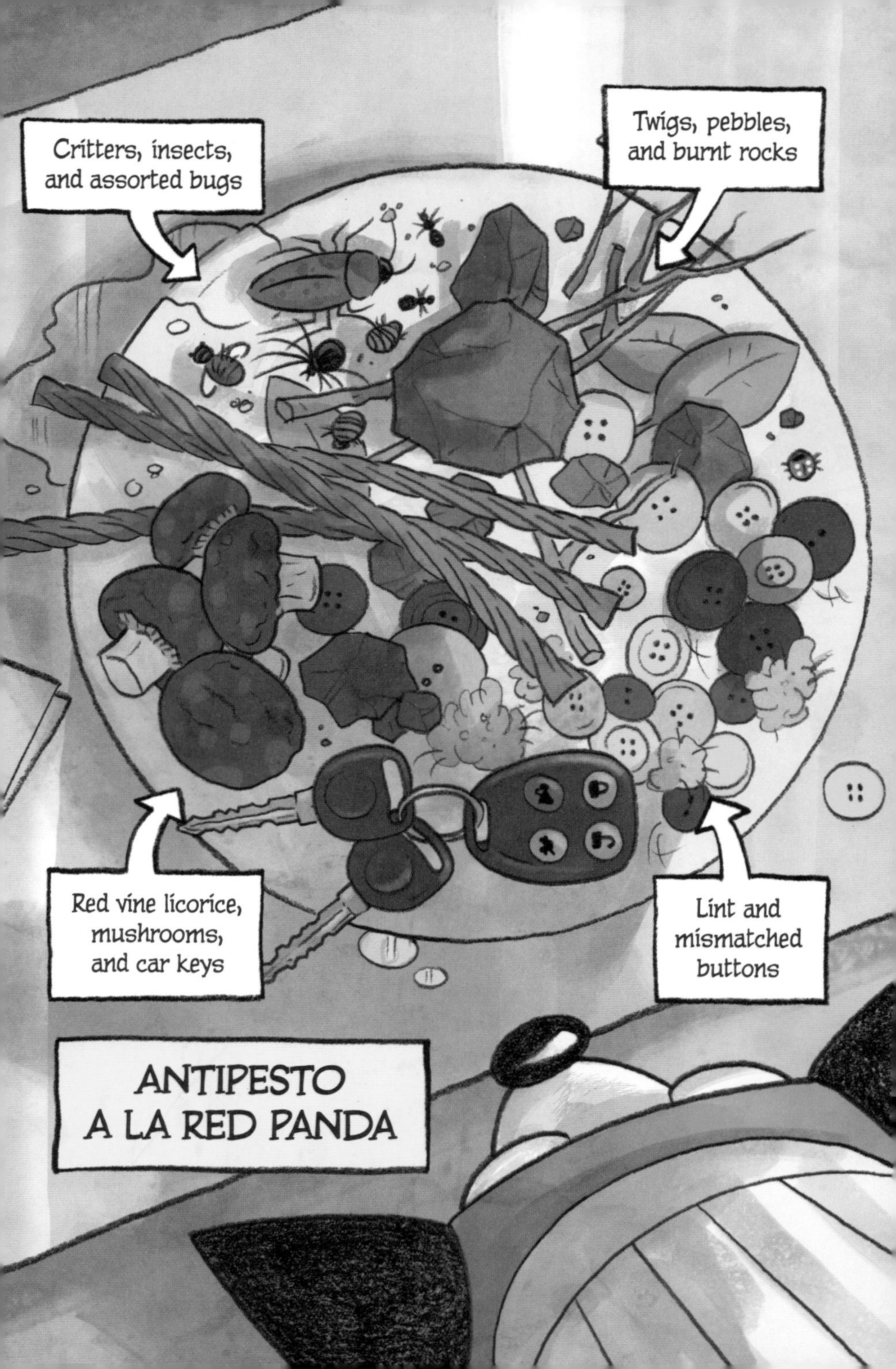
Critters, insects, and assorted bugs
Twigs, pebbles, and burnt rocks
Red vine licorice, mushrooms, and car keys
Lint and mismatched buttons
ANTIPESTO A LA RED PANDA

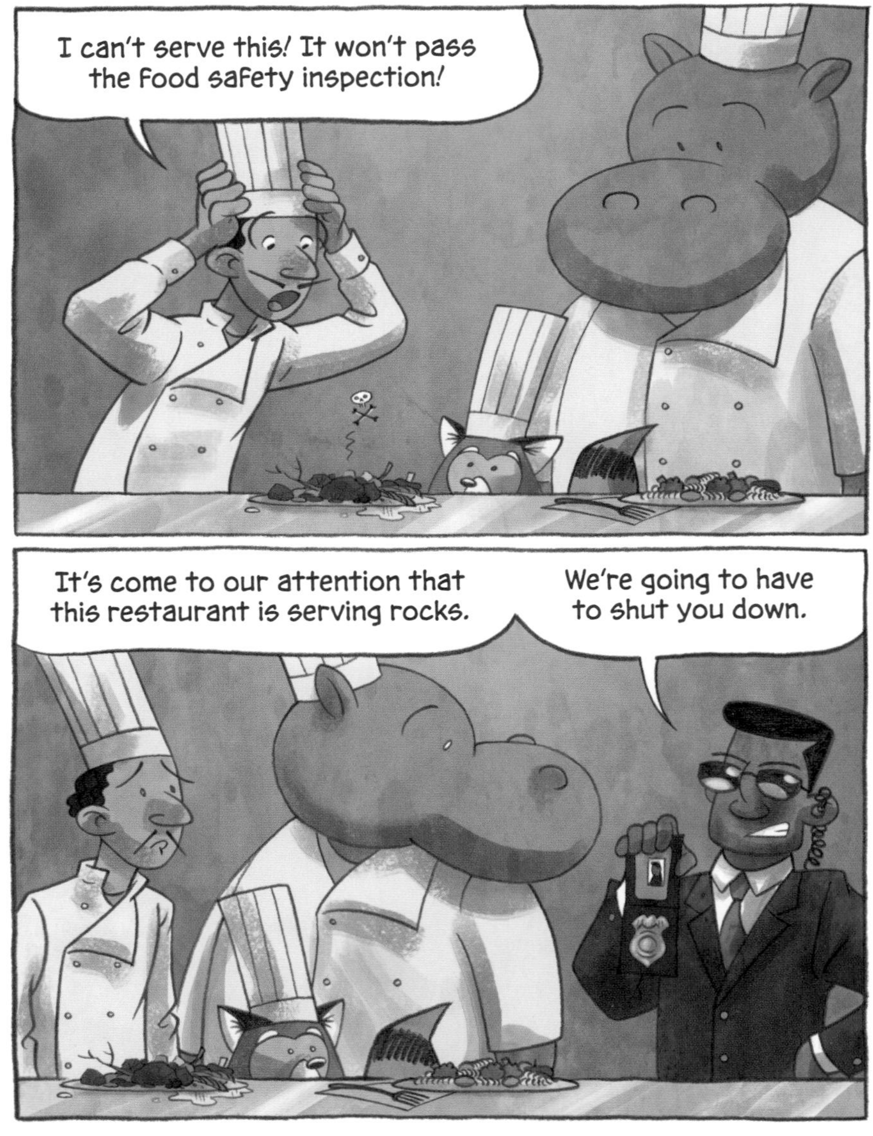
I can't serve this! It won't pass the food safety inspection!
It's come to our attention that this restaurant is serving rocks.
We're going to have to shut you down.

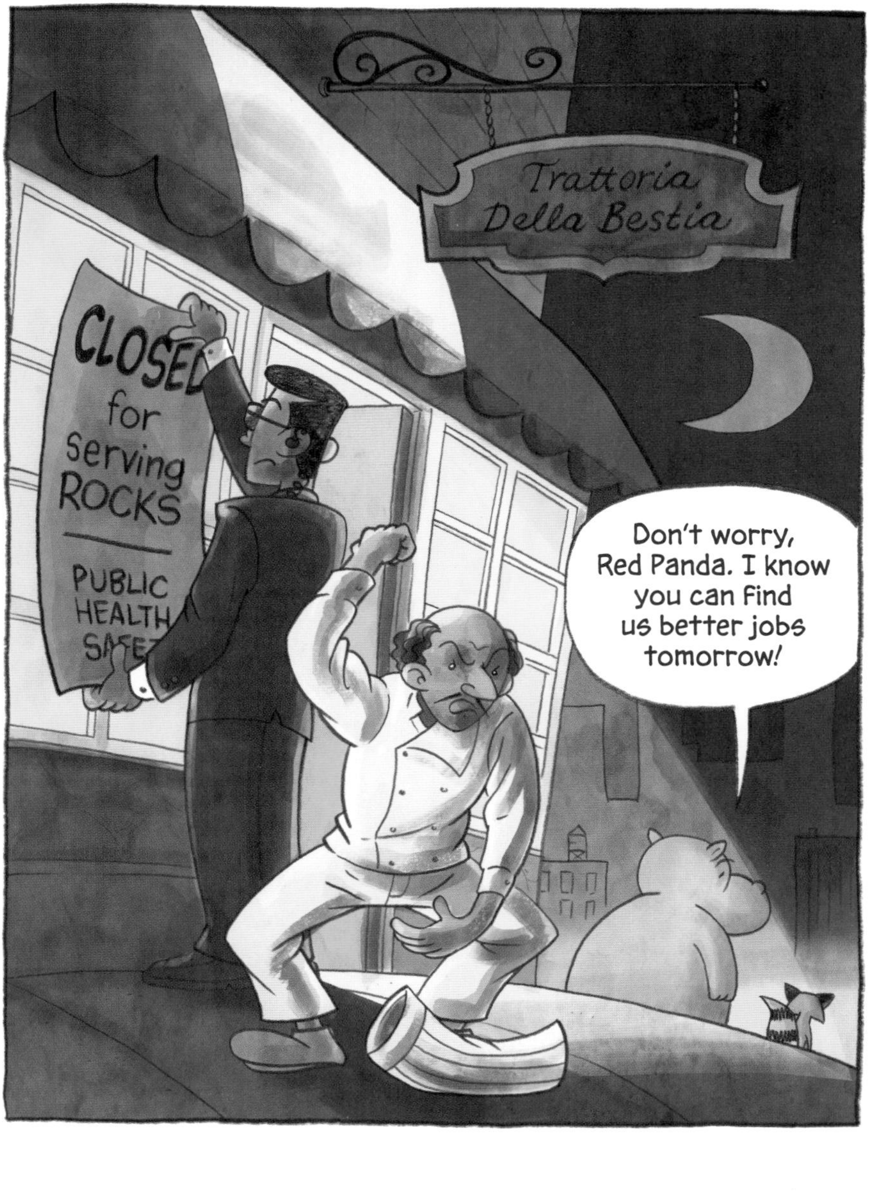
Trattoria
Della Bestia
CLOSED
for
serving
ROCKS
PUBLIC
HEALTH
Don't worry, Red Panda. I know you can find us better jobs tomorrow!

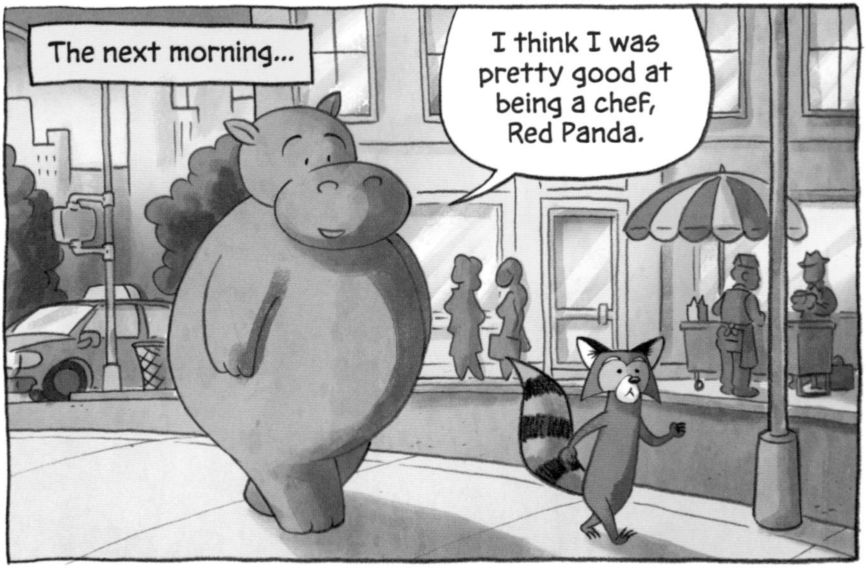
The next morning...
I think I was pretty good at being a chef, Red Panda.

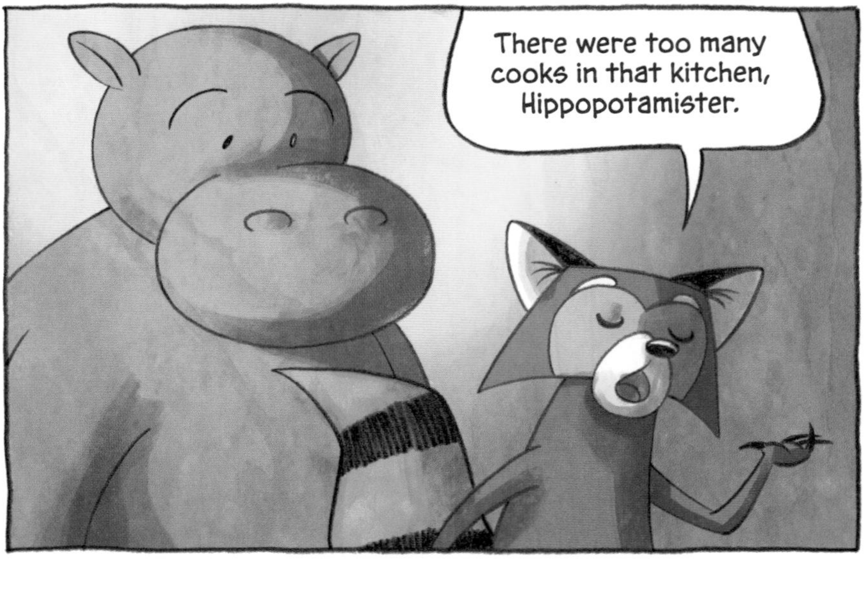
There were too many cooks in that kitchen, Hippopotamister.

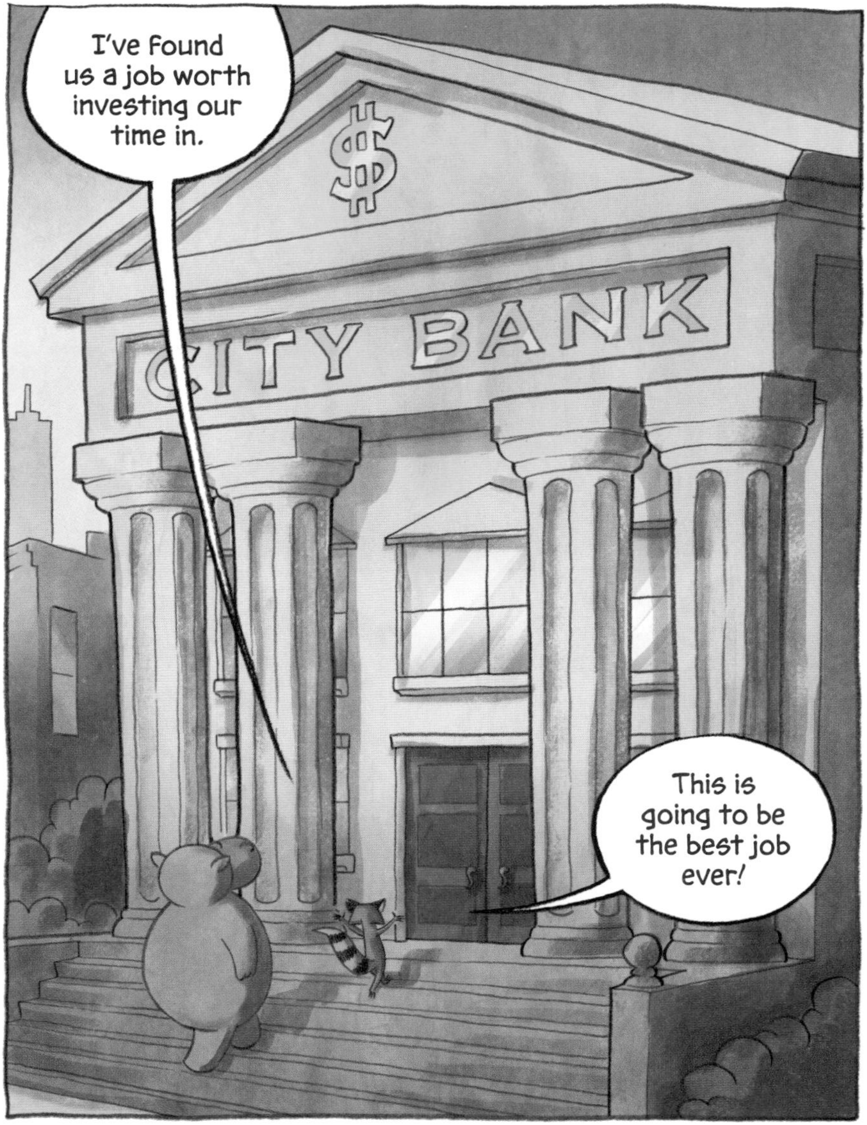
I've found us a job worth investing our time in.
$
CITY BANK
This is going to be the best job ever!

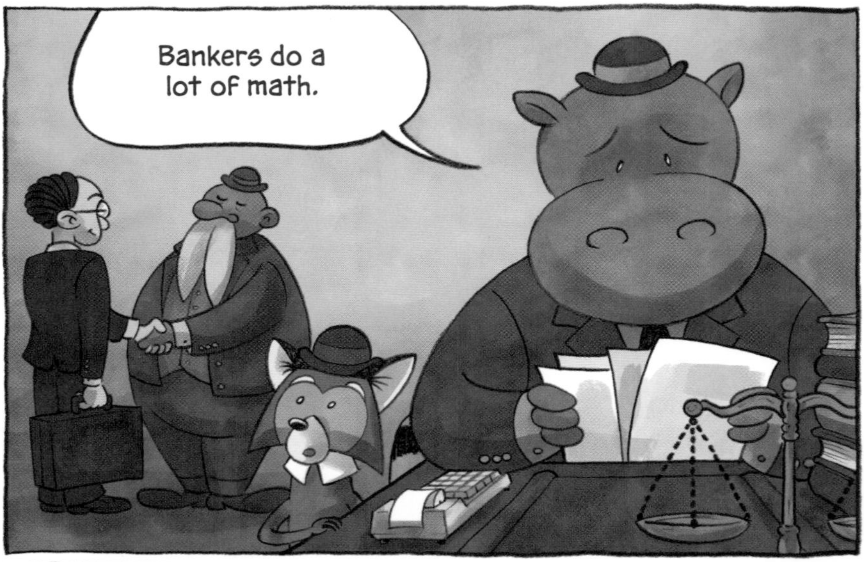
Bankers do a lot of math.

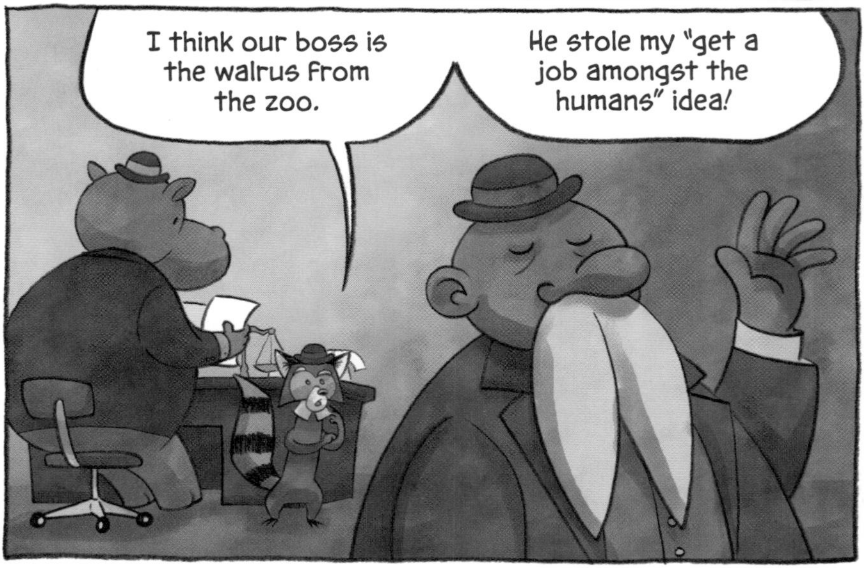
I think our boss is the walrus from the zoo.
He stole my "get a job amongst the humans" idea!

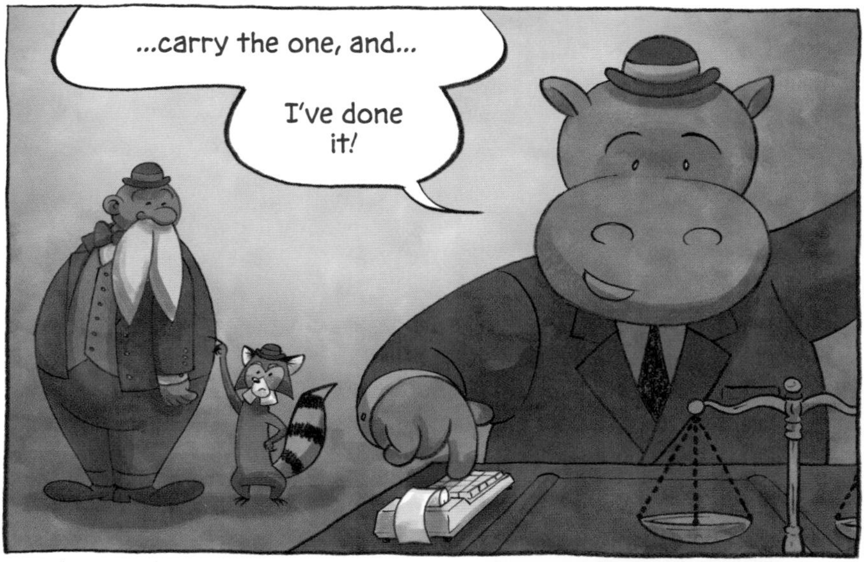
...carry the one, and...
I've done it!

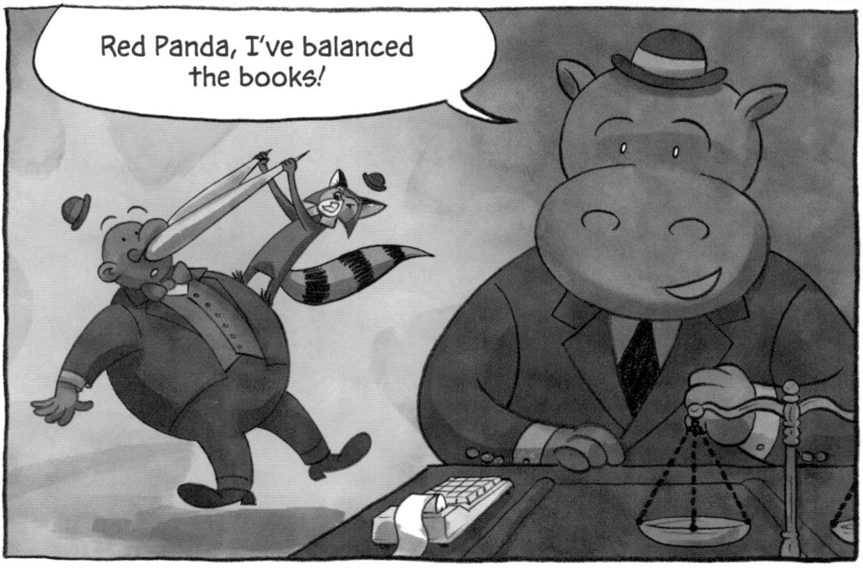
Red Panda, I've balanced the books!

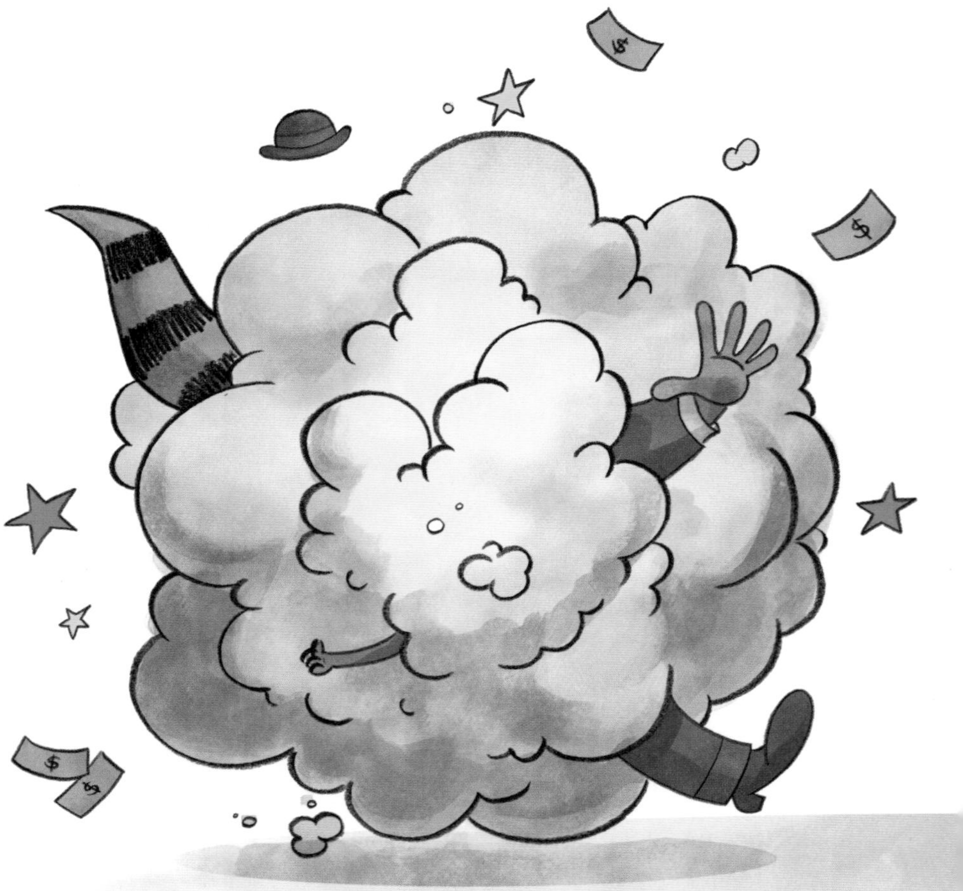

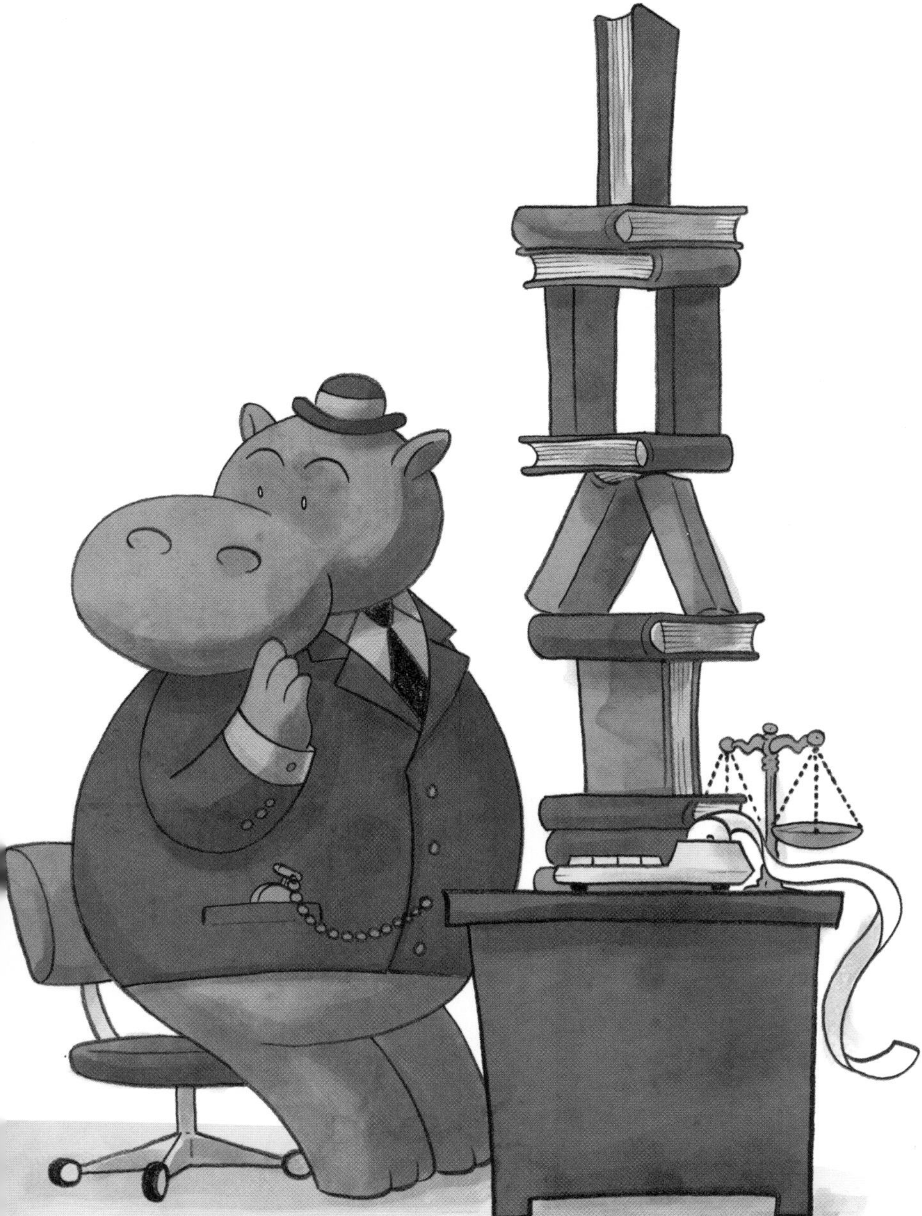

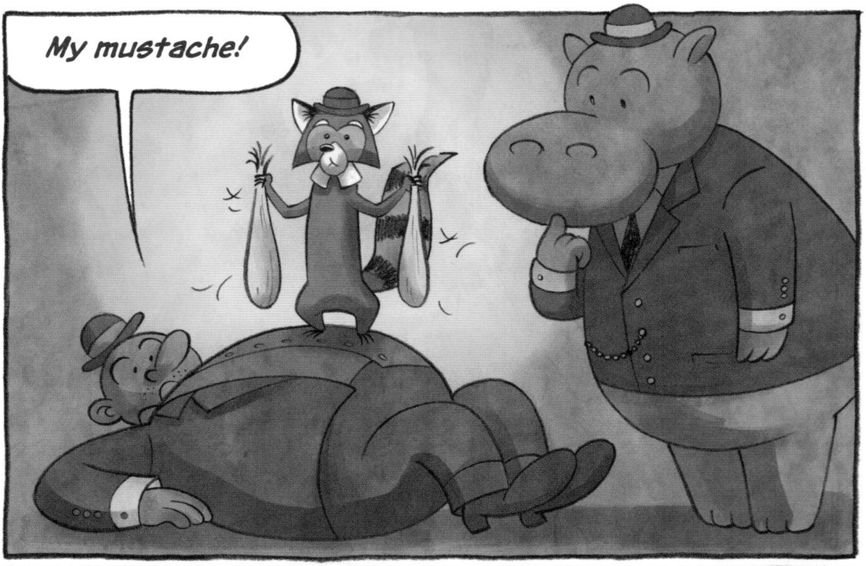
My mustache!

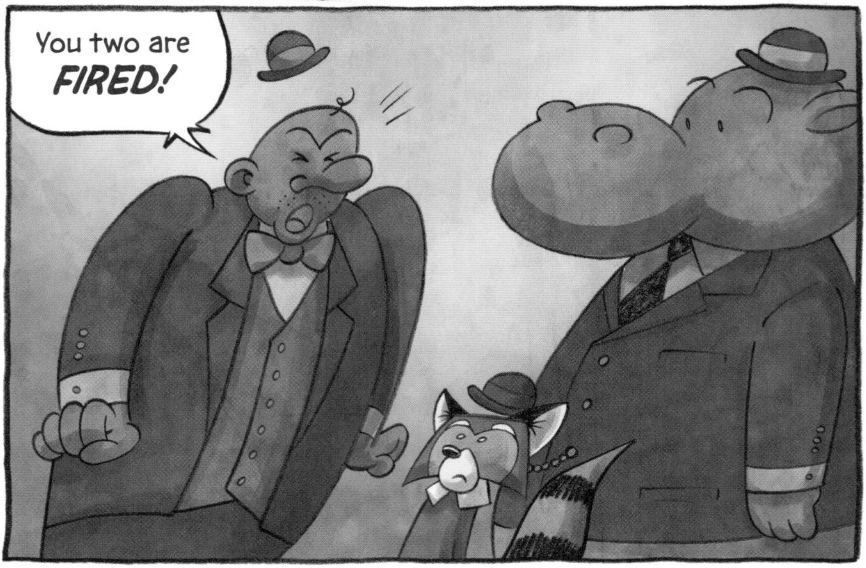
You two are FIRED!

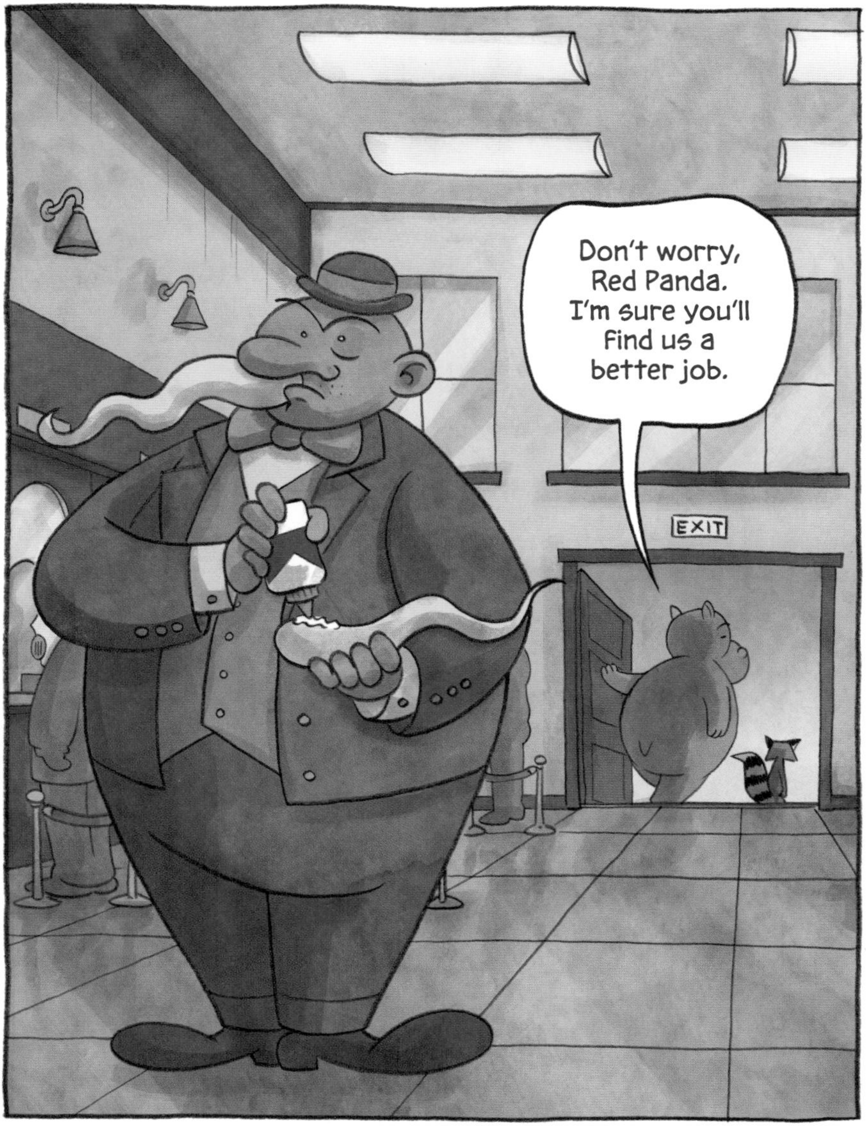
Don't worry, Red Panda. I'm sure you'll find us a better job.
EXIT

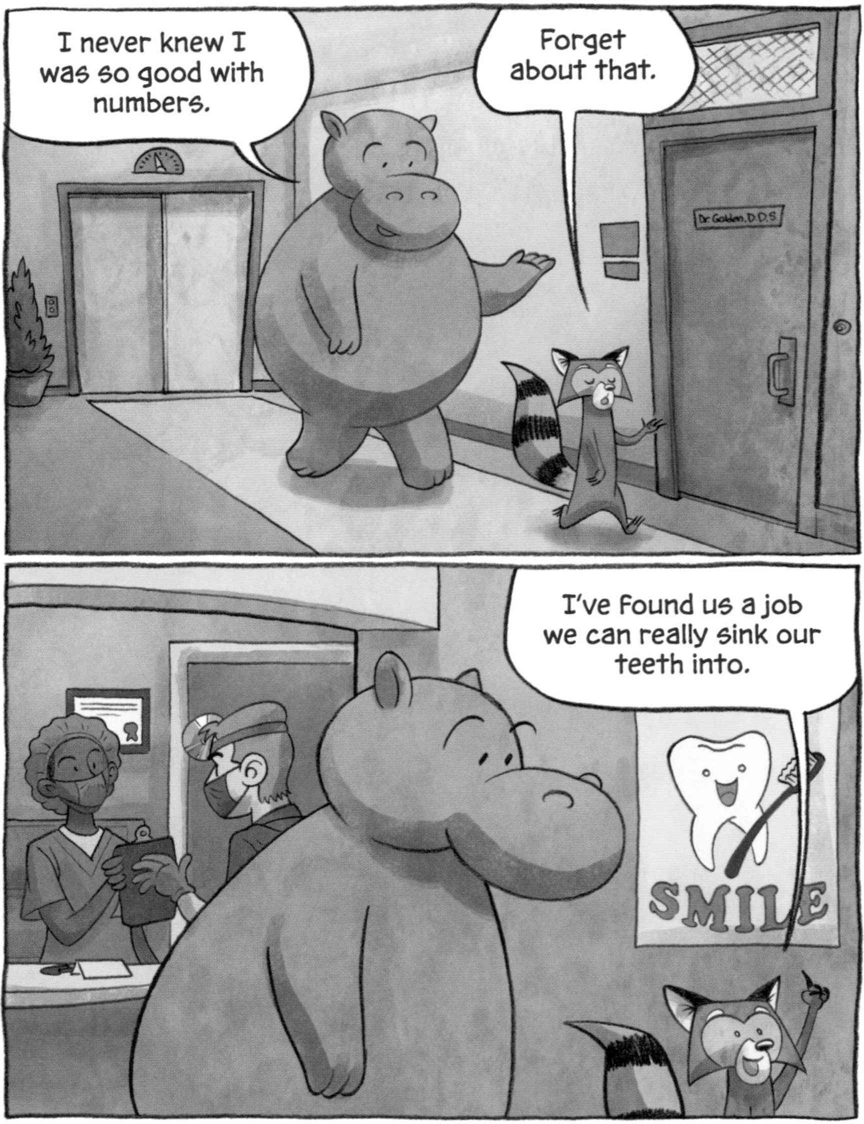
I never knew I was so good with numbers.
Forget about that.
Dr. Golden, D.D.S.
I've found us a job we can really sink our teeth into.
SMILE

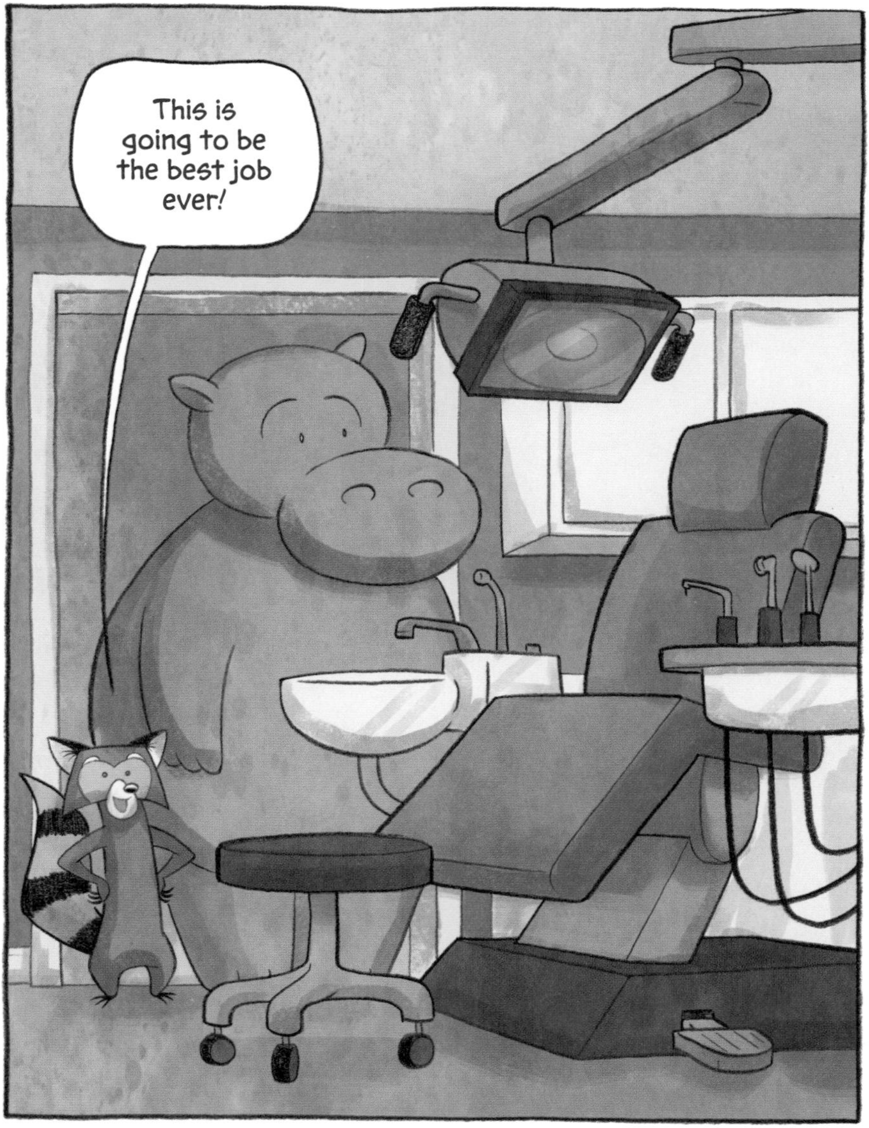
This is going to be the best job ever!

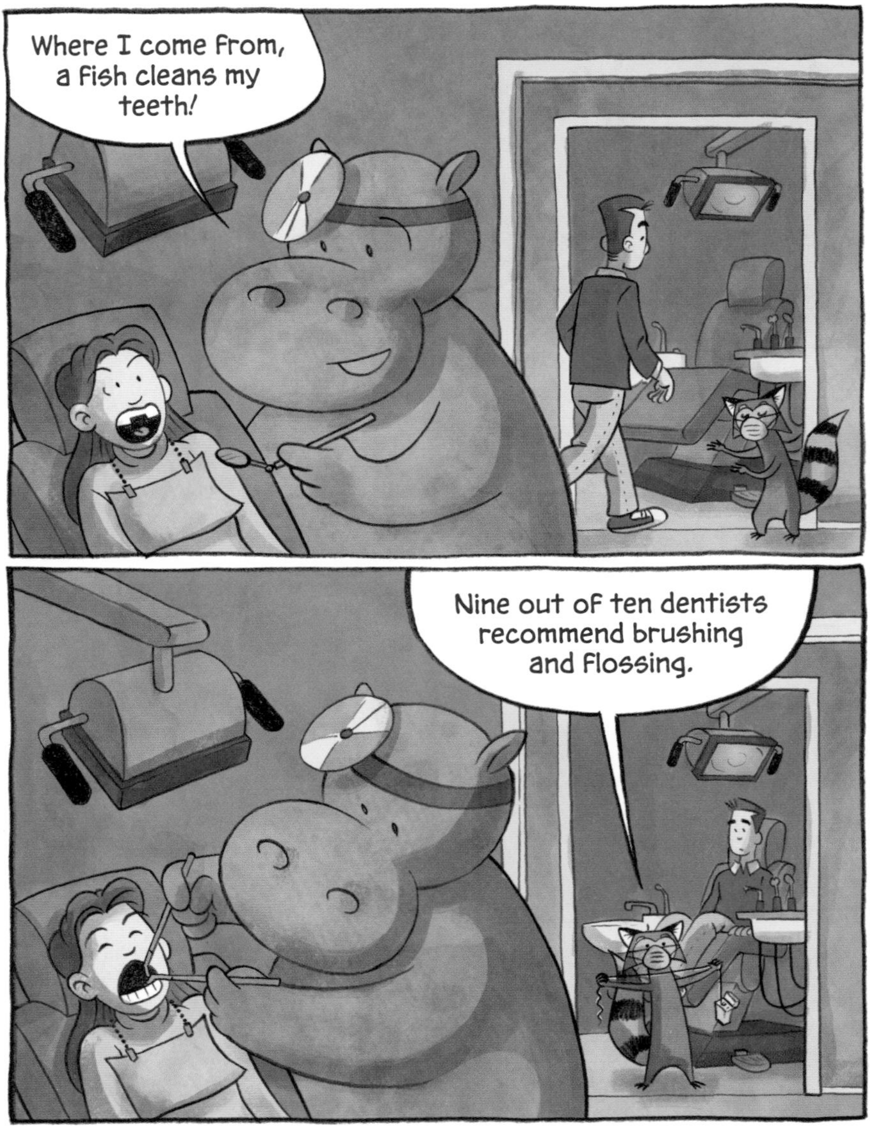
Where I come from, a fish cleans my teeth!
Nine out of ten dentists recommend brushing and flossing.

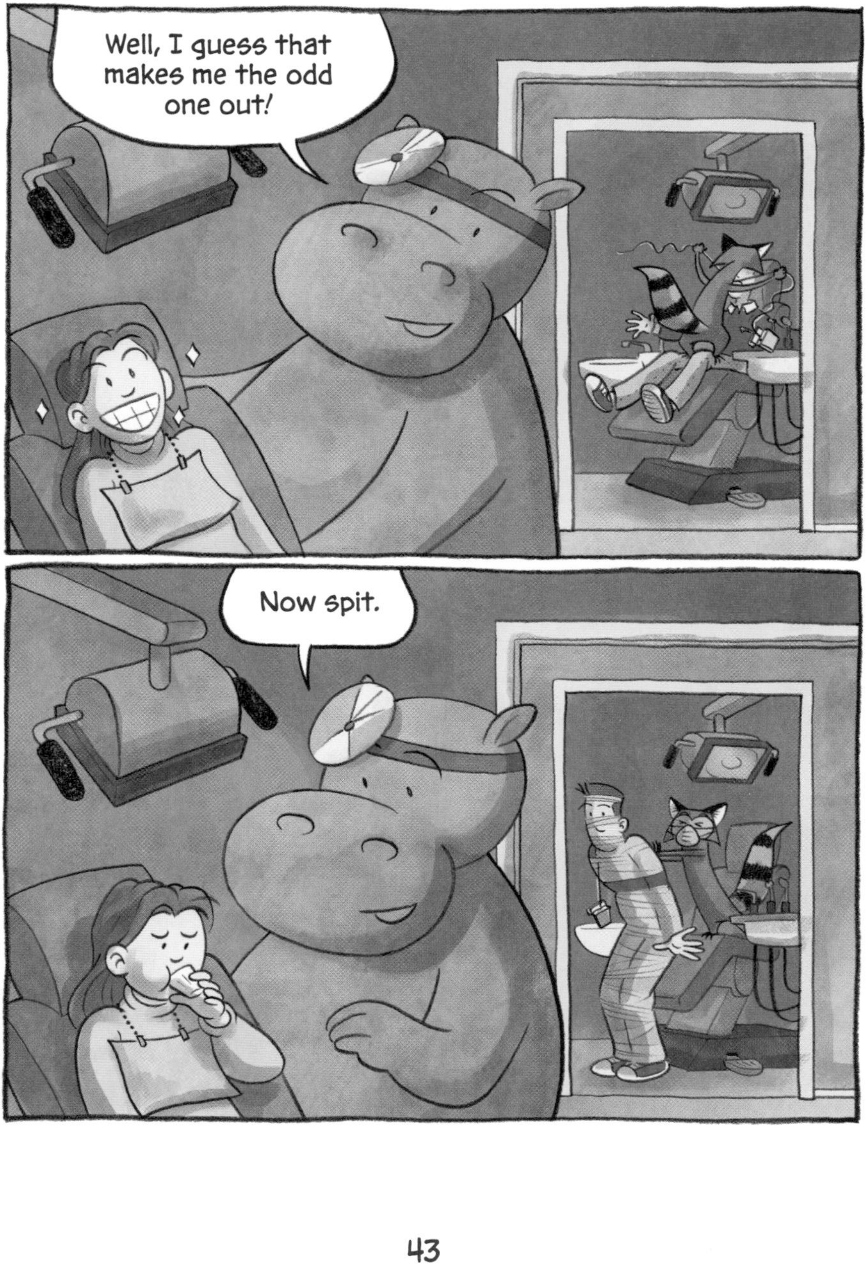
Well, I guess that makes me the odd one out!
Now spit.

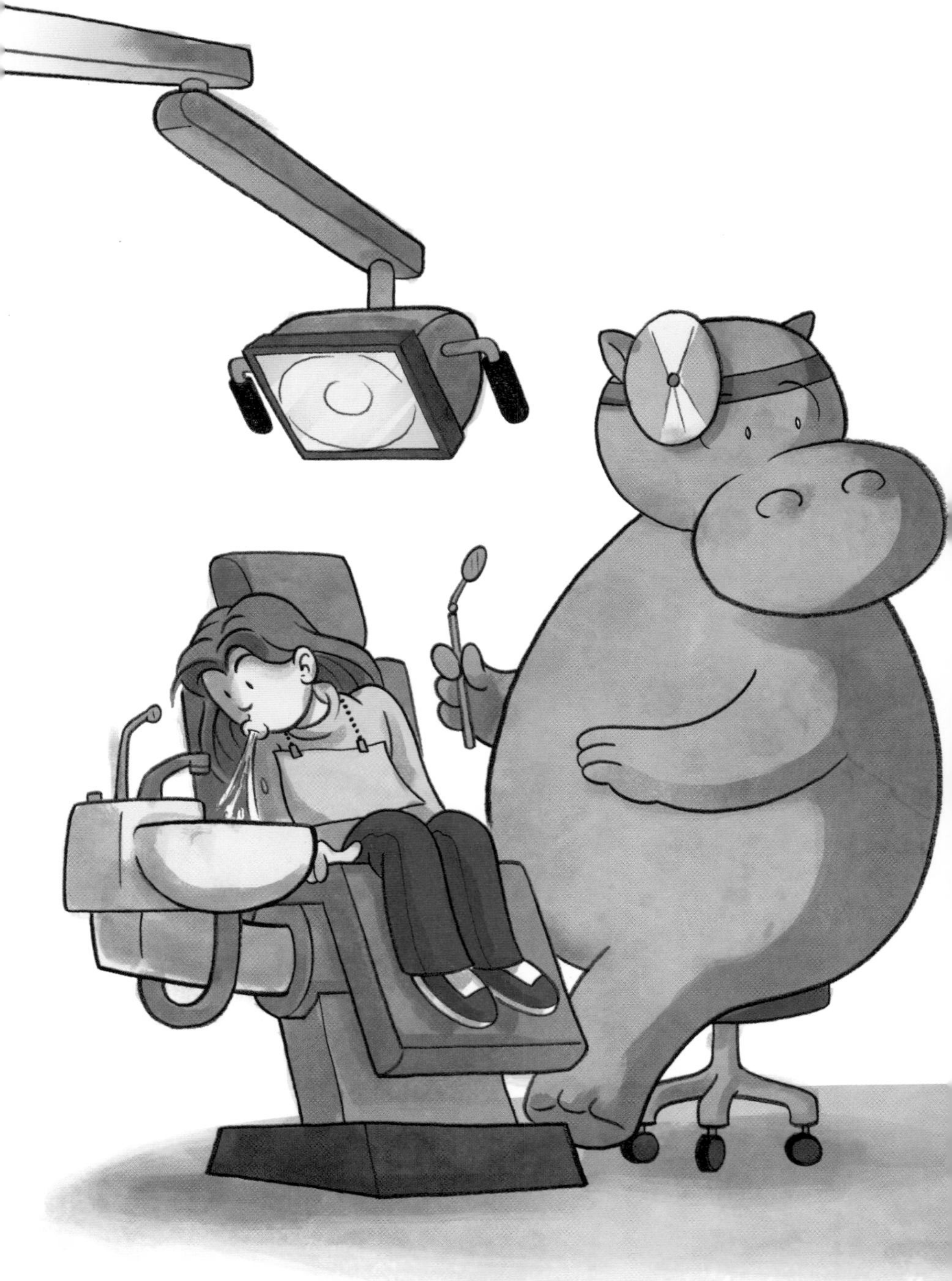

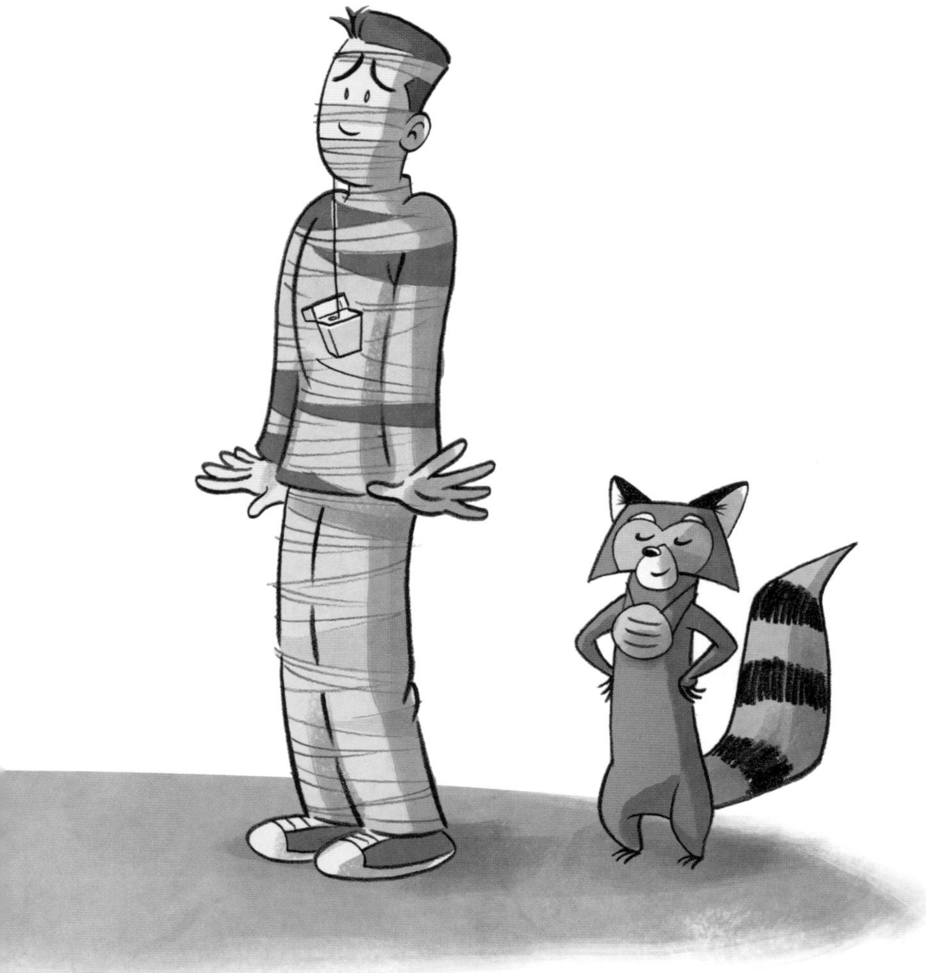

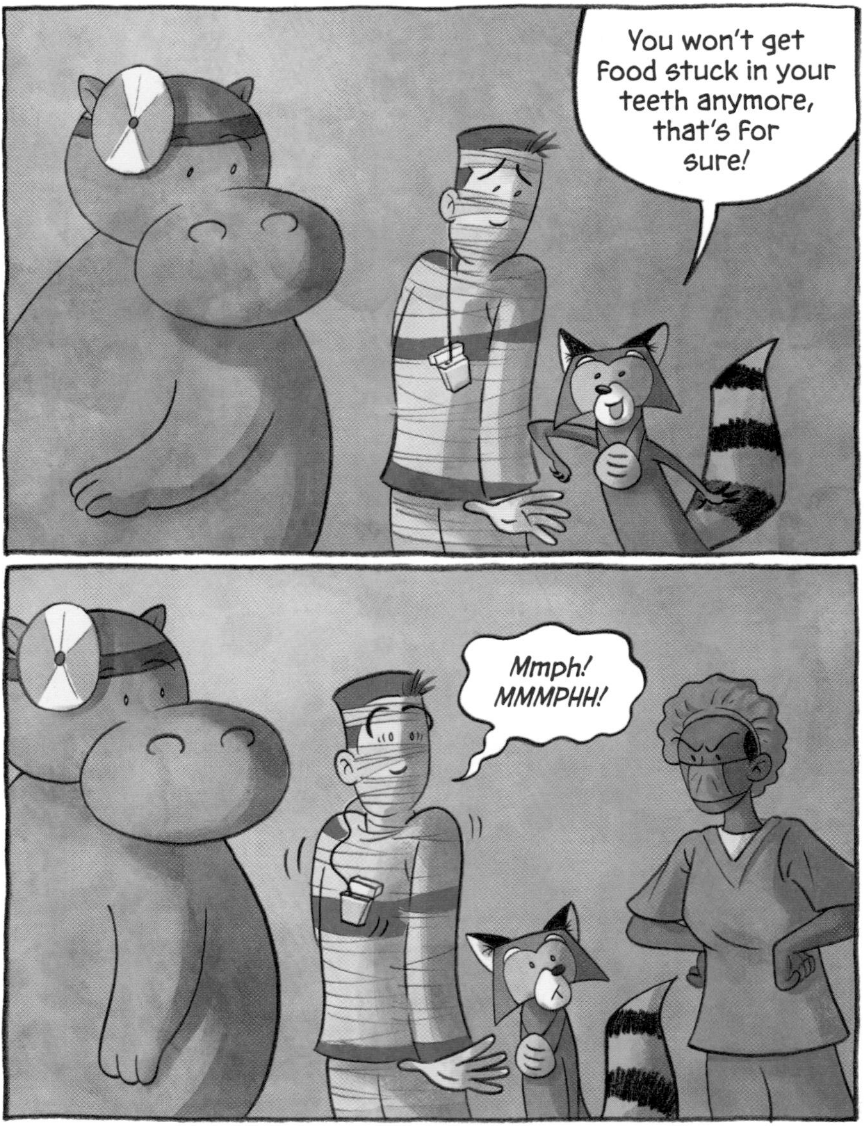
You won't get food stuck in your teeth anymore, that's for sure!
Mmph! MMMPHH!

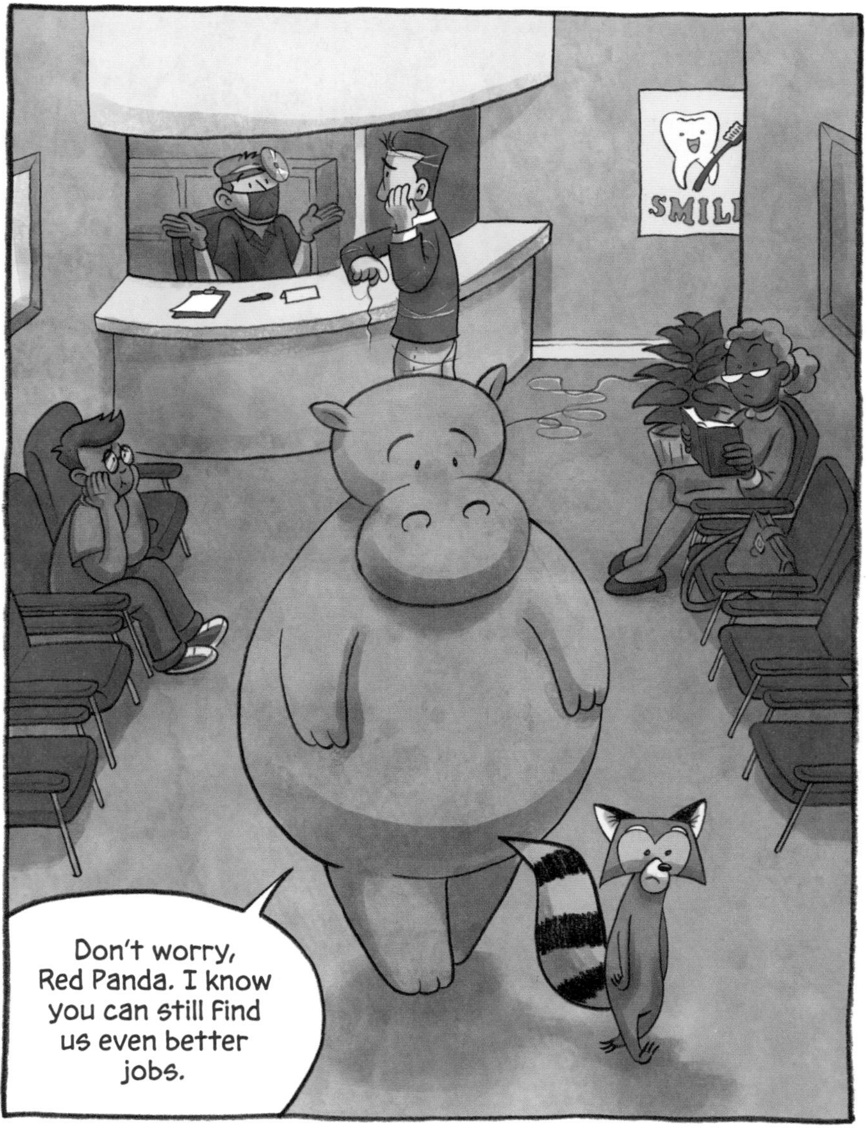
SMILE
Don't worry, Red Panda. I know you can still find us even better jobs.

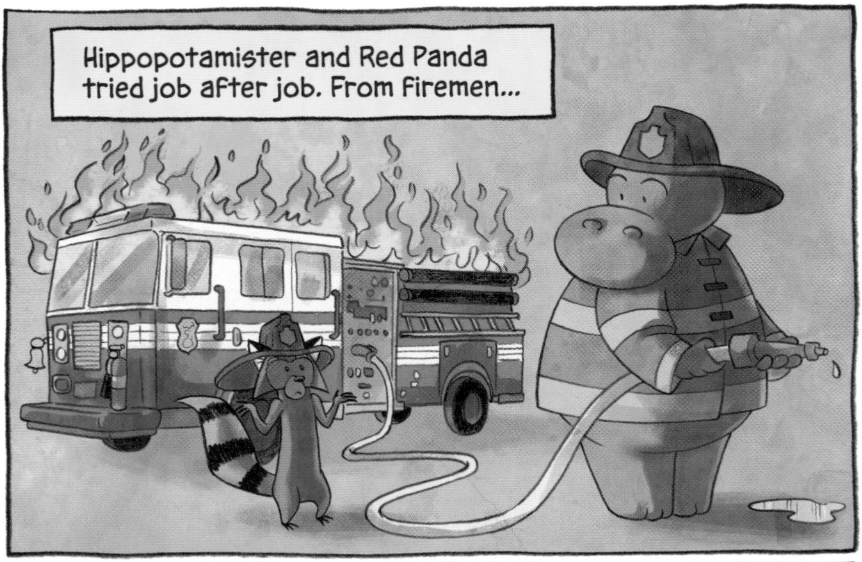
Hippopotamister and Red Panda tried job after job. From firemen...

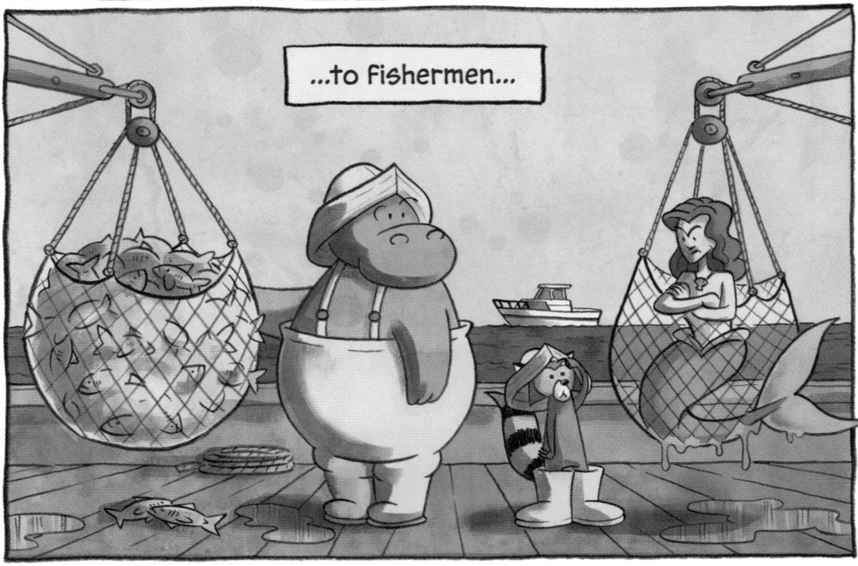
...to fishermen...

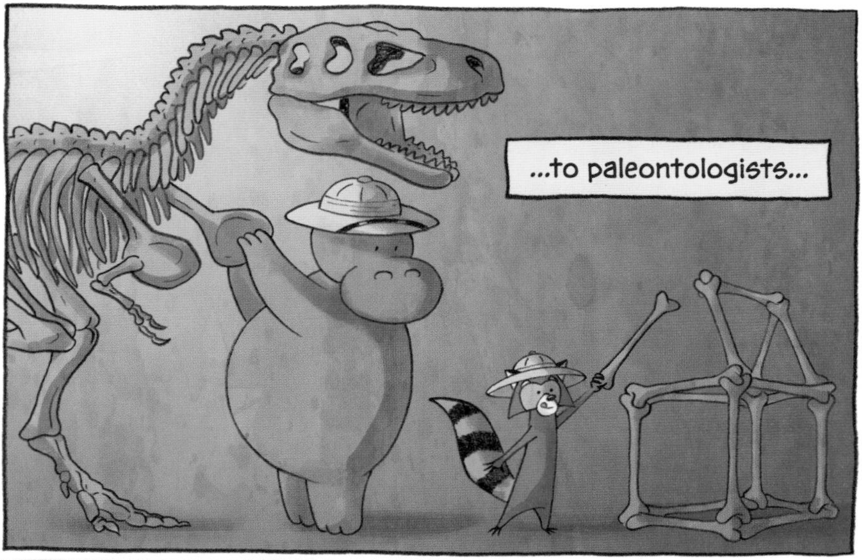
...to paleontologists...

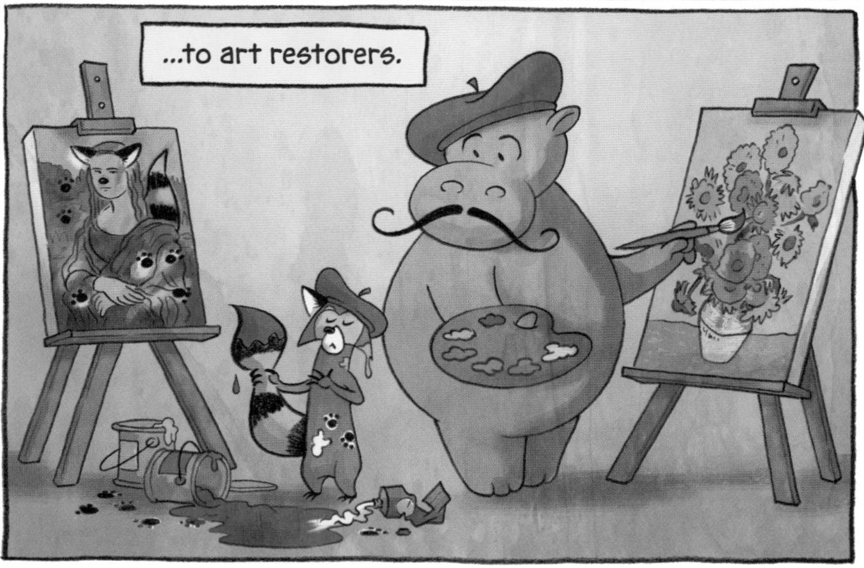
...to art restorers.

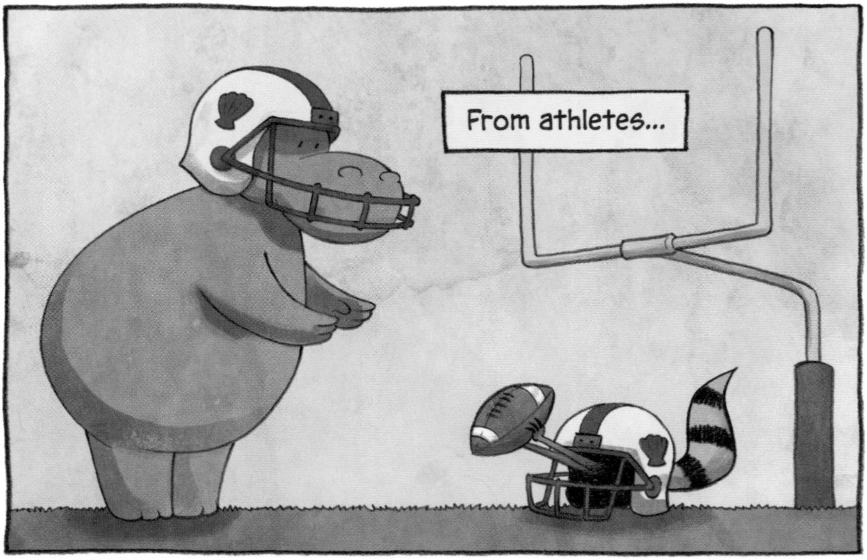
From athletes...

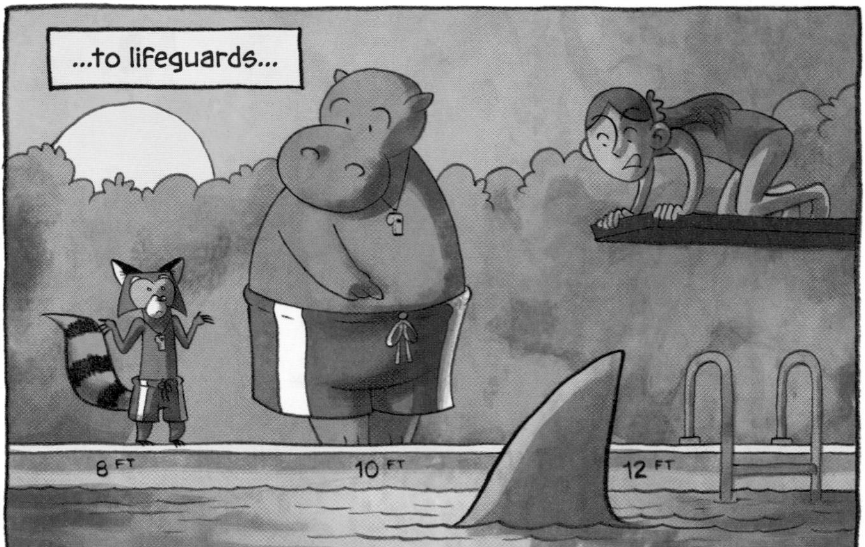
...to lifeguards...
8 FT
10 FT
12 FT

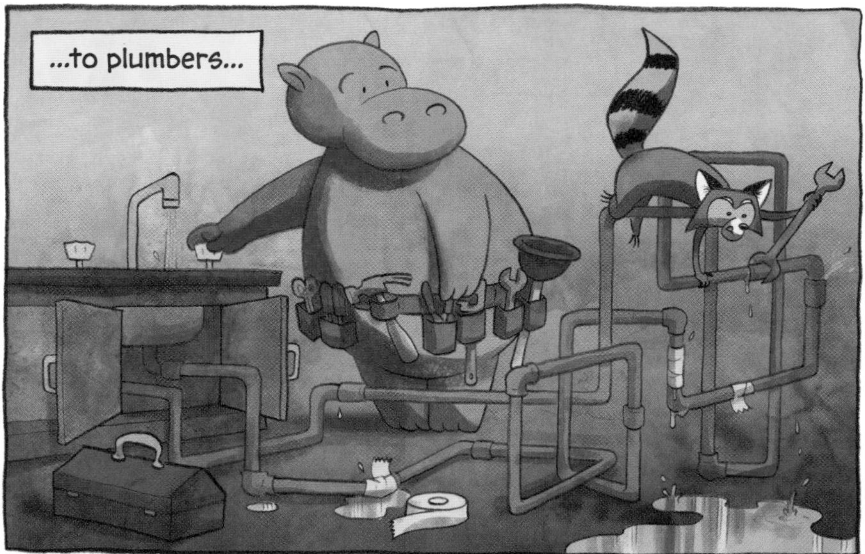
...to plumbers...

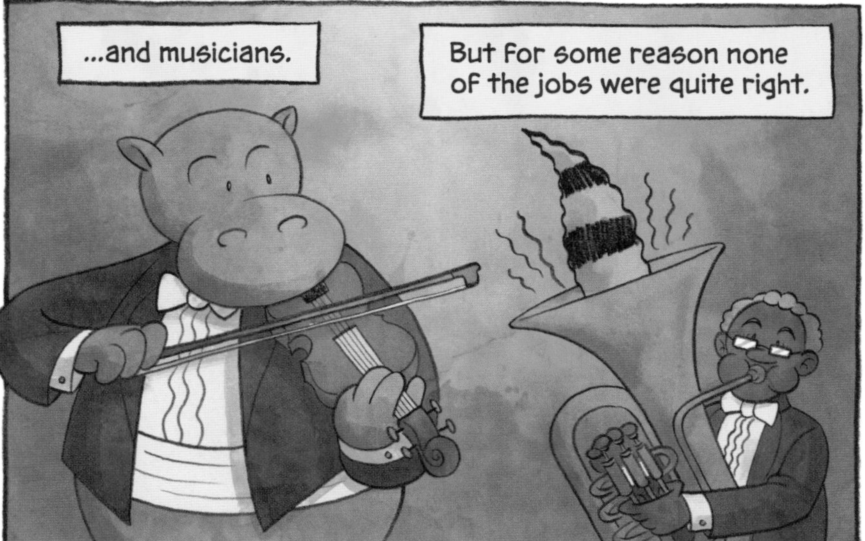
...and musicians.
But for some reason none of the jobs were quite right.

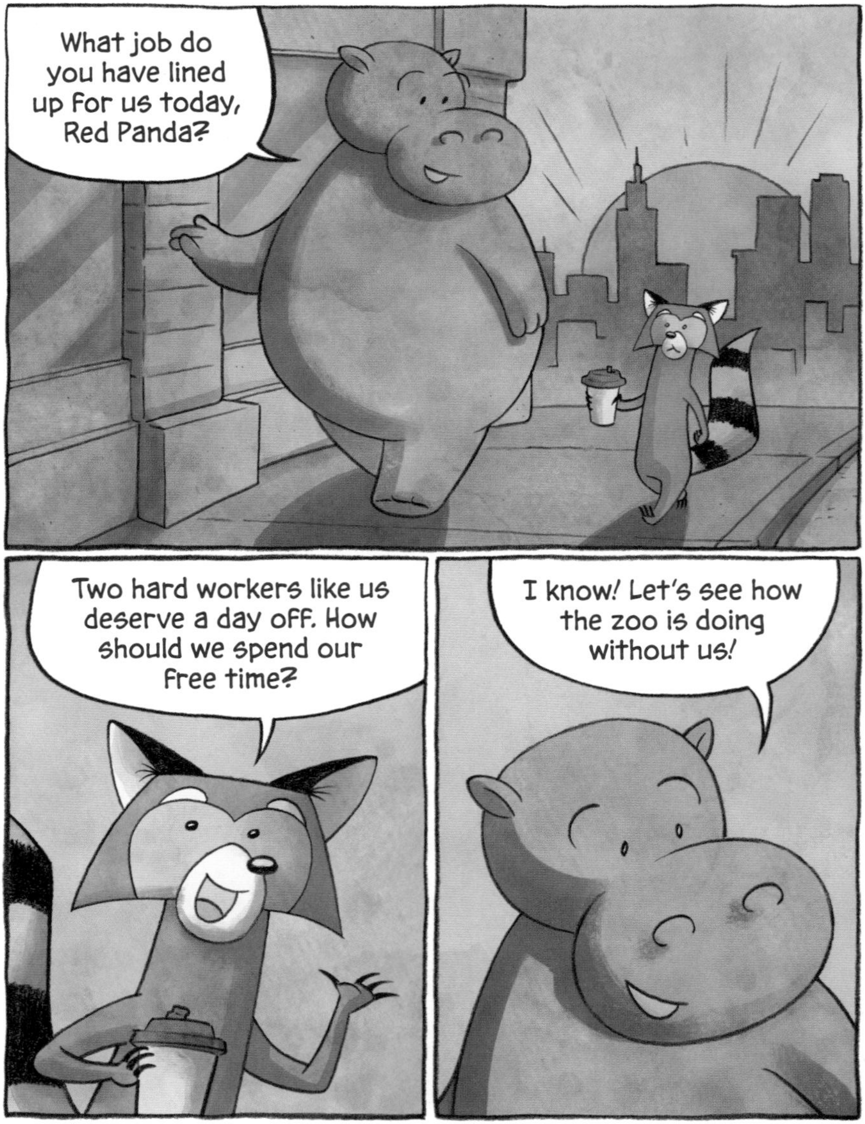
What job do you have lined up for us today, Red Panda?
Two hard workers like us deserve a day off. How should we spend our free time?
I know! Let's see how the zoo is doing without us!

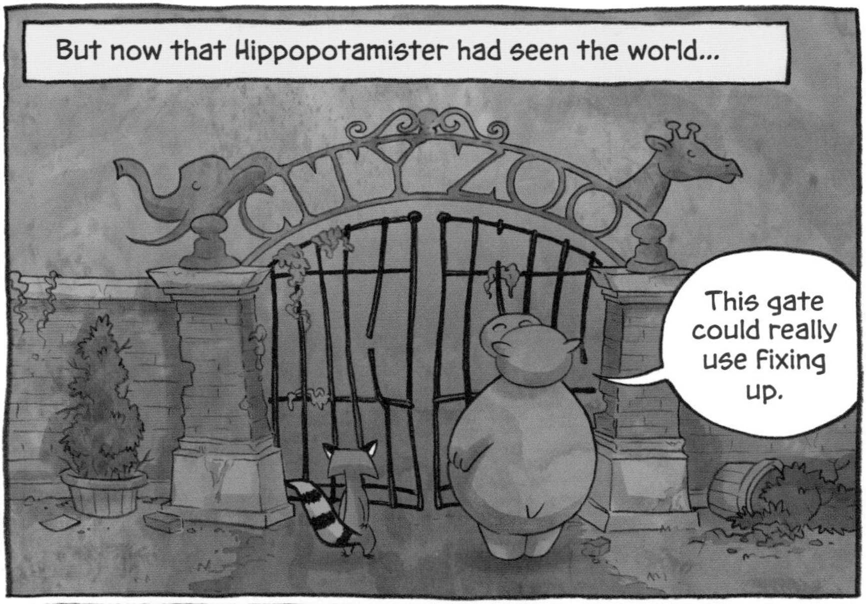
But now that Hippopotamister had seen the world...
CITY ZOO
This gate could really use fixing up.

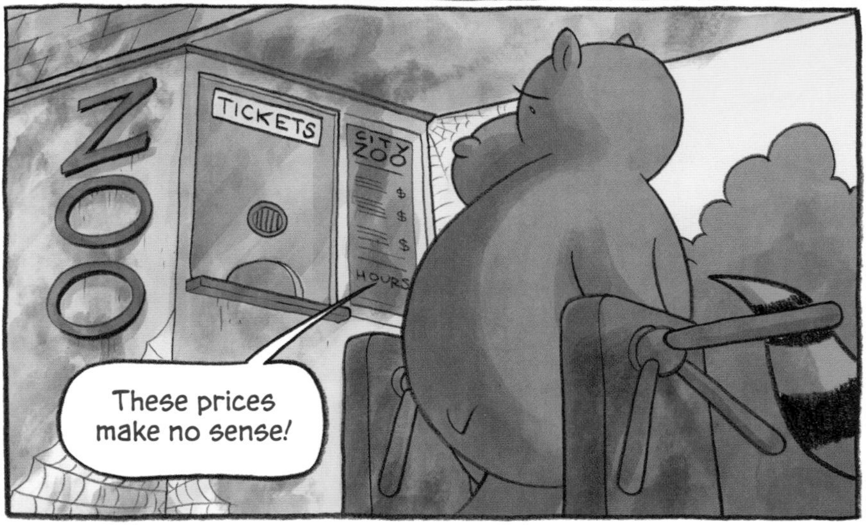
ZOO
TICKETS
CITY ZOO
$
$
$
HOURS
These prices make no sense!

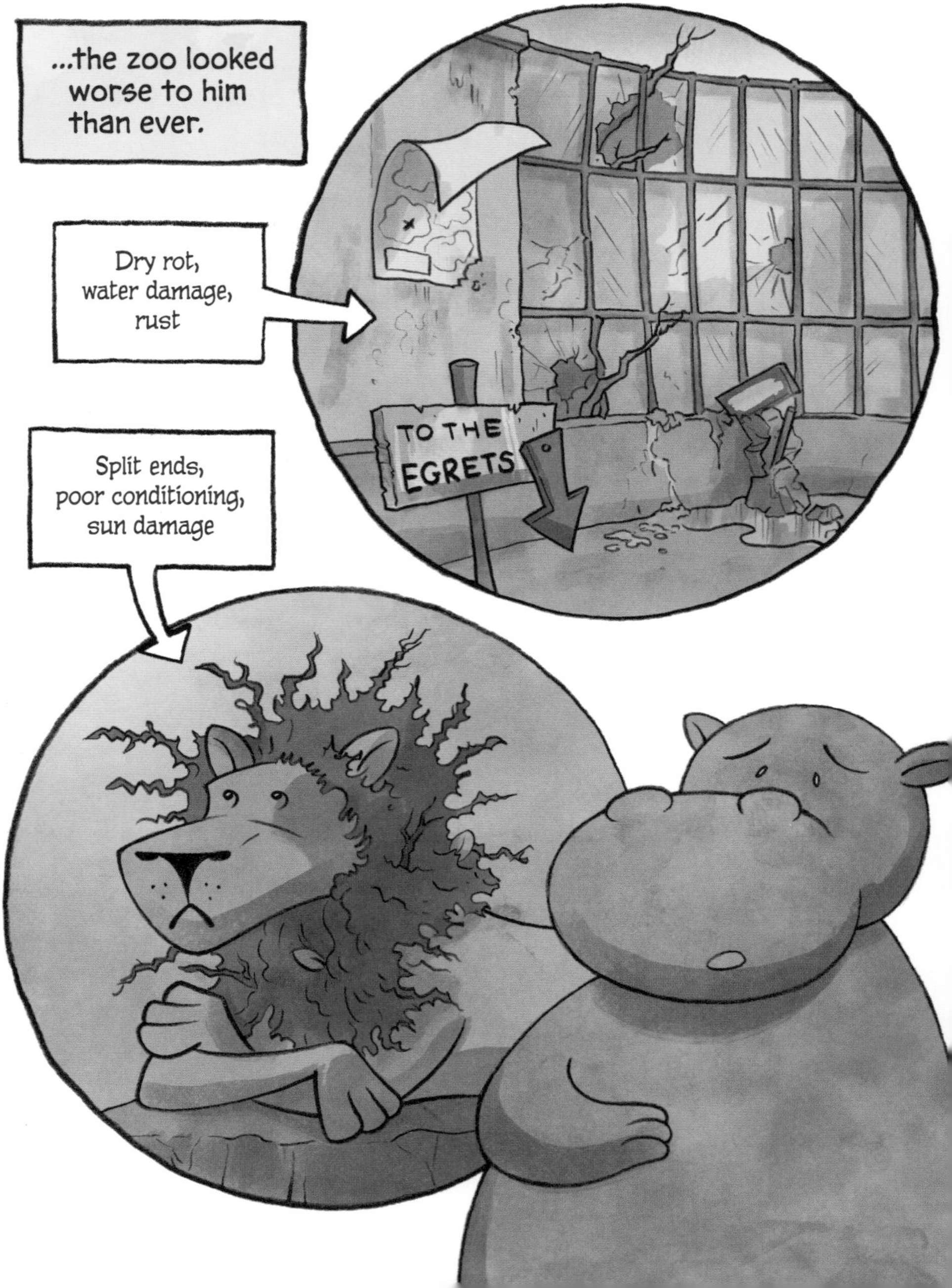
...the zoo looked worse to him than ever.
Dry rot, water damage, rust
TO THE EGRETS
Split ends, poor conditioning, sun damage

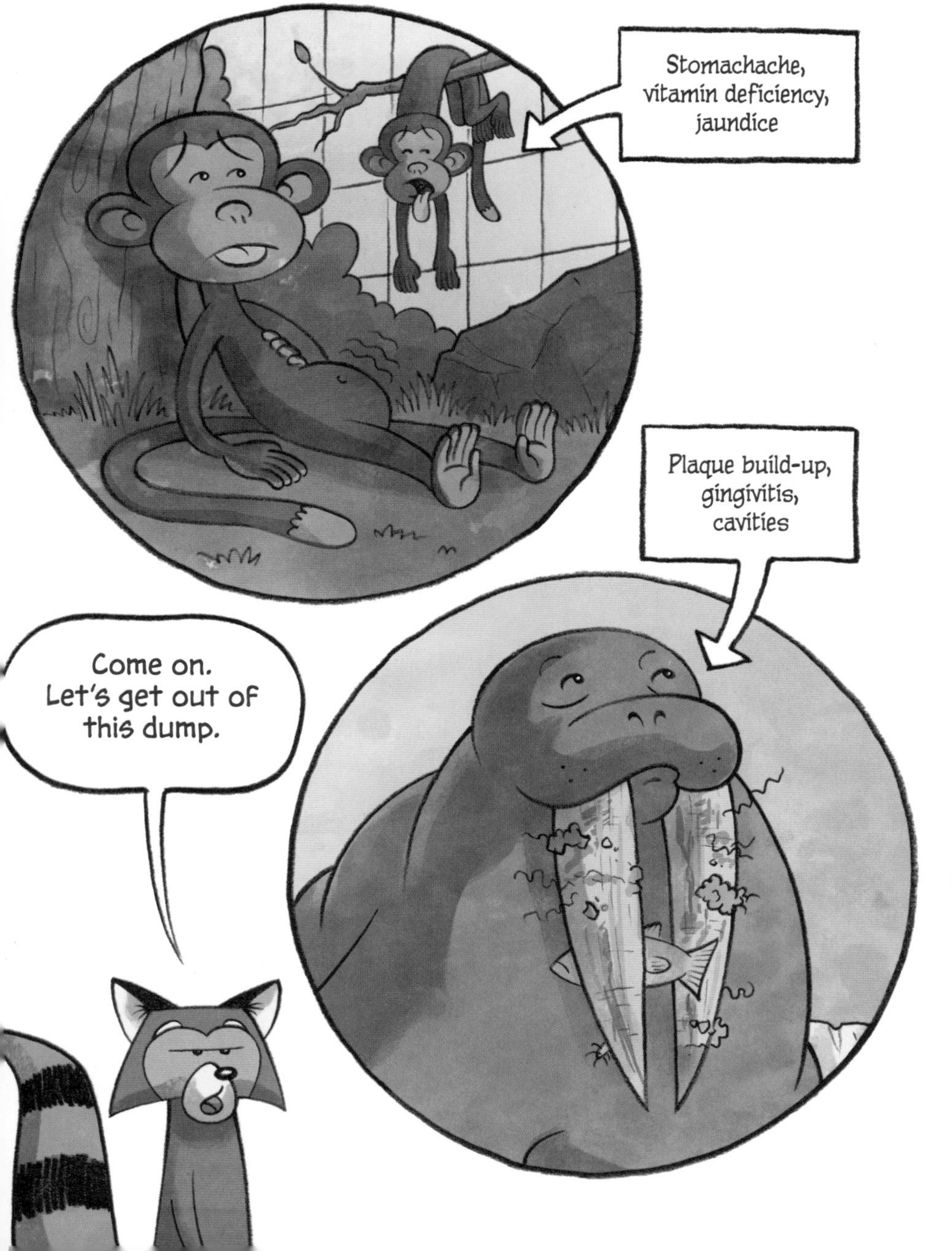
Stomachache, vitamin deficiency, jaundice
Plaque build-up, gingivitis, cavities
Come on. Let's get out of this dump.

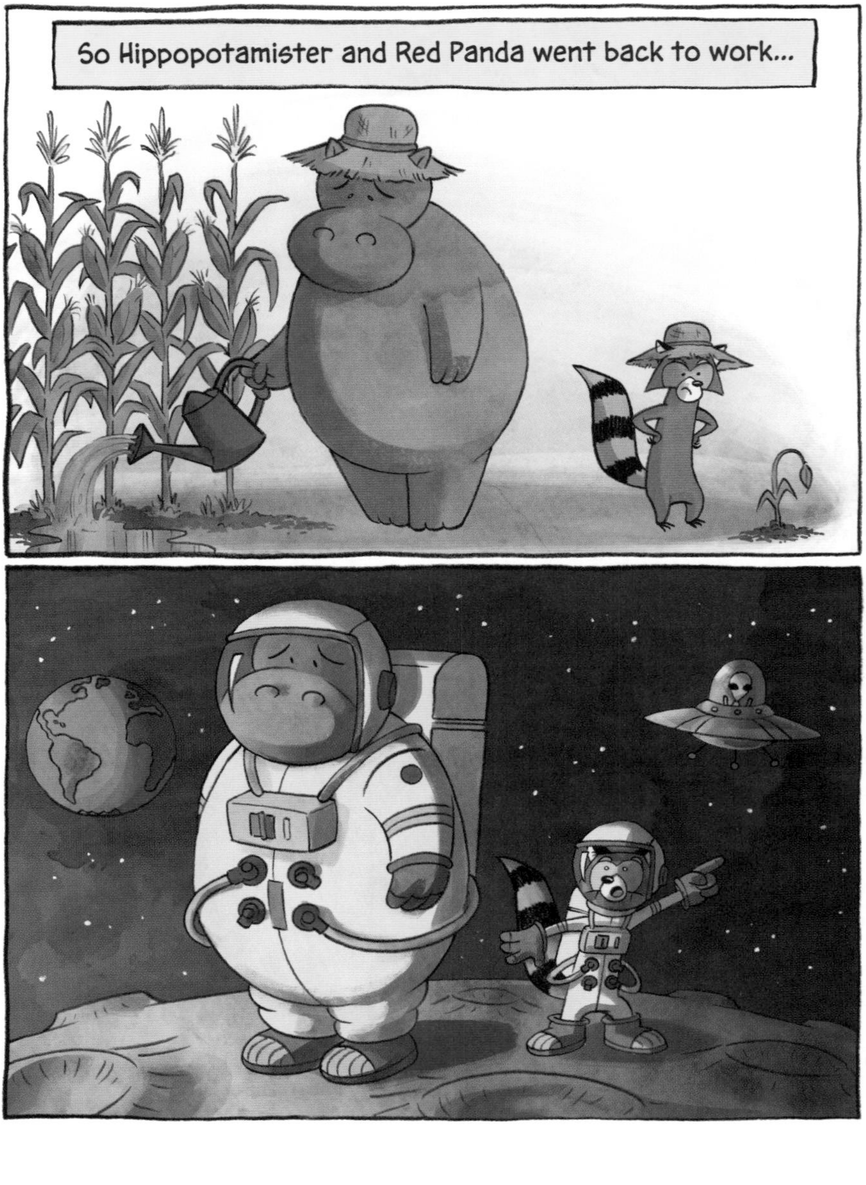
So Hippopotamister and Red Panda went back to work...

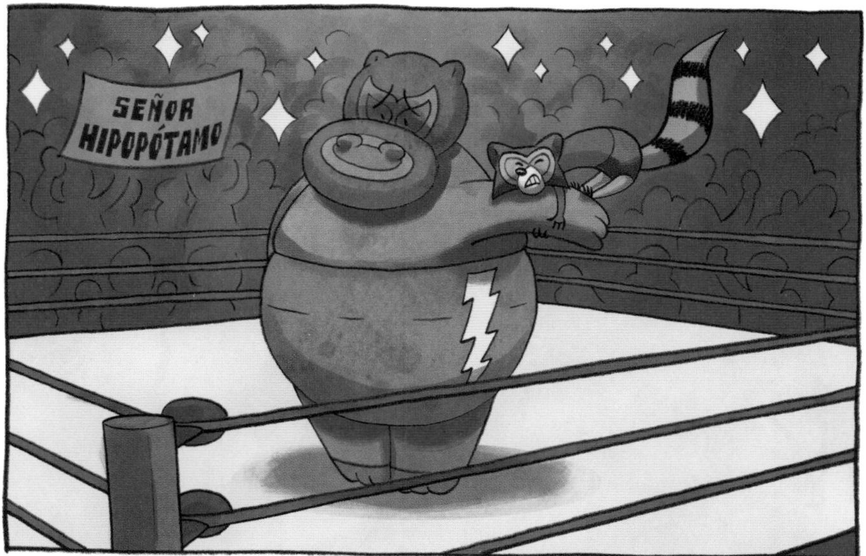
SEÑOR
HIPOPÓTAMO

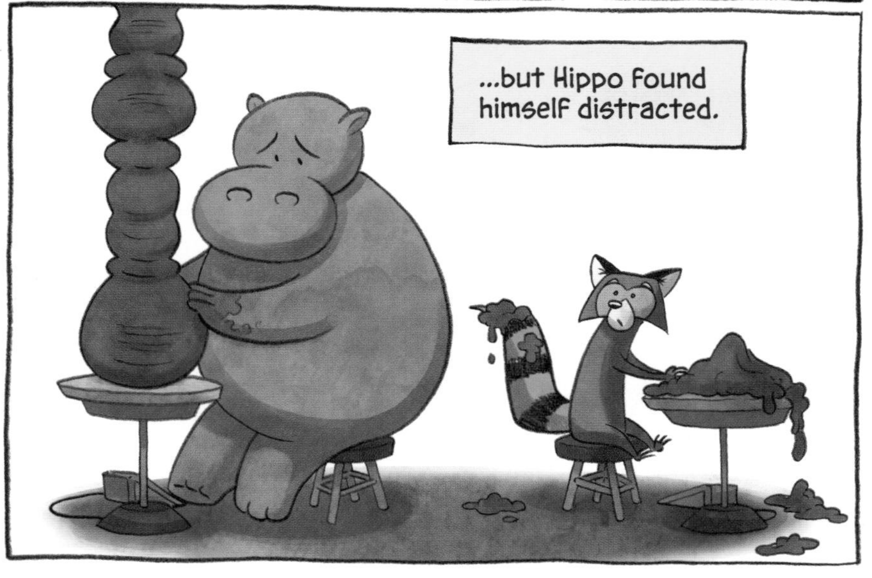
...but Hippo found
himself distracted.

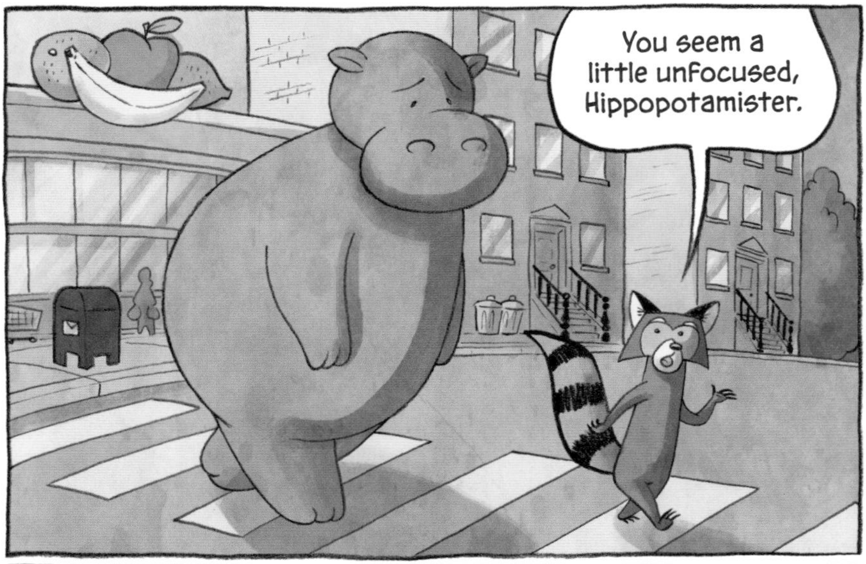
You seem a little unfocused, Hippopotamister.

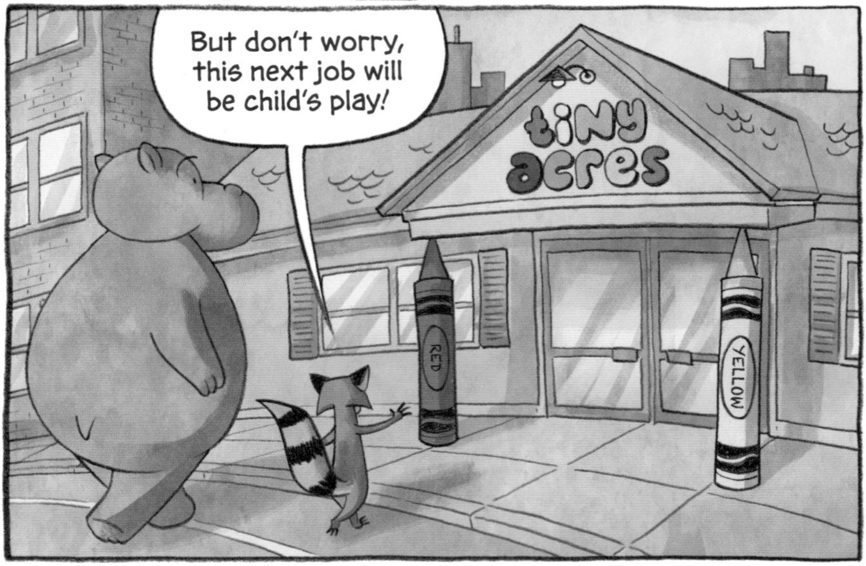
But don't worry, this next job will be child's play!
tiny acres
RED
YELLOW

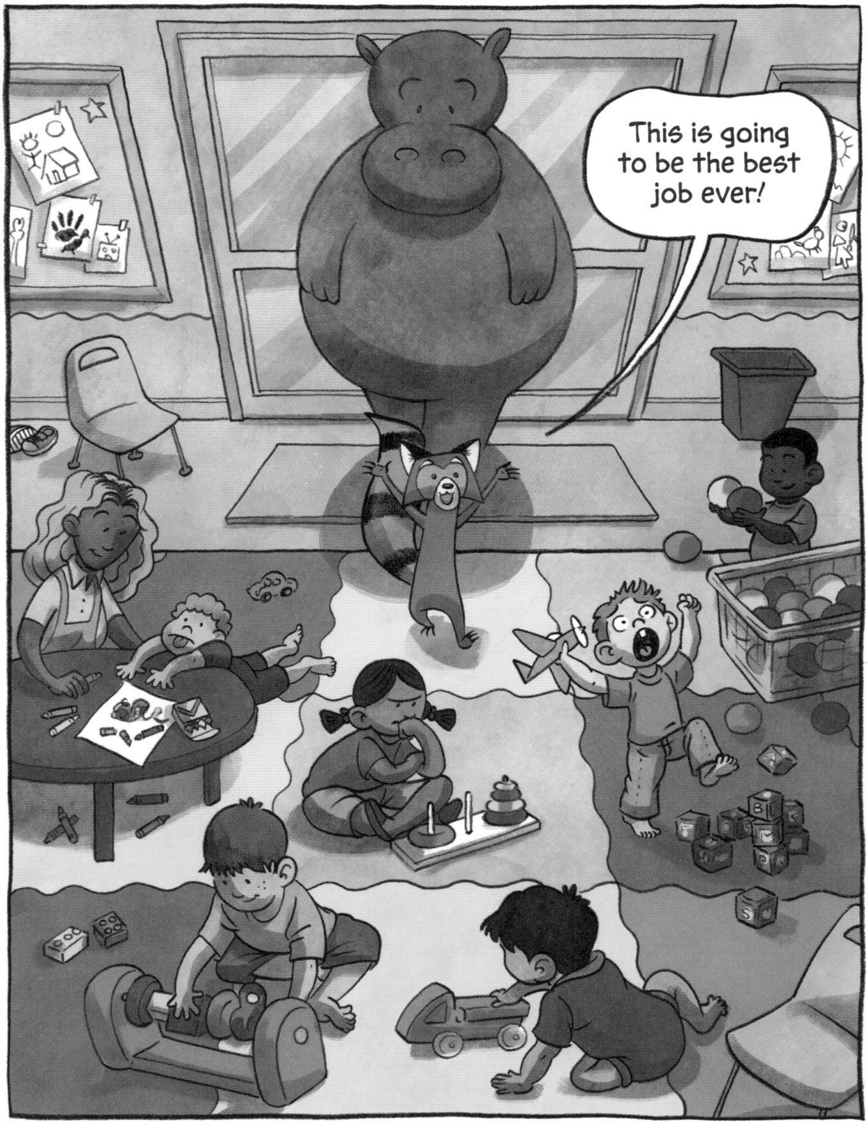
This is going to be the best job ever!

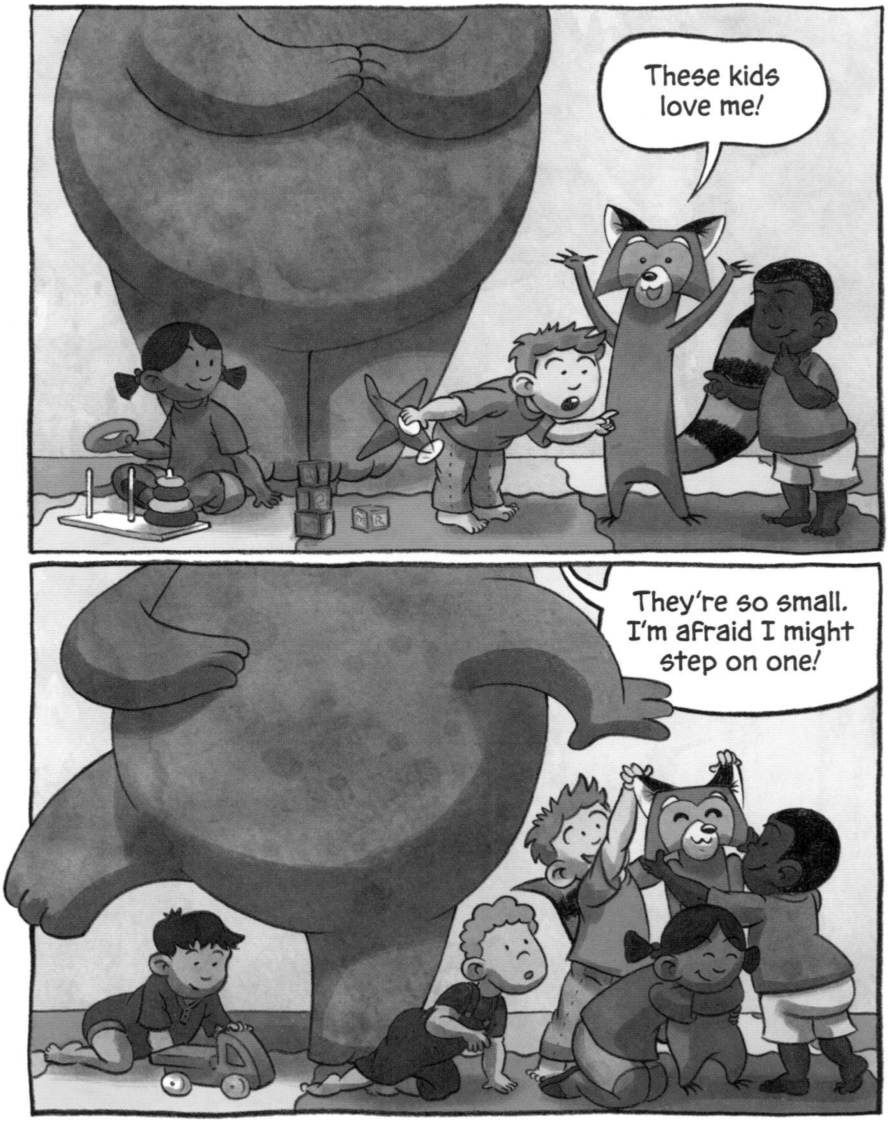
These kids love me!
They're so small. I'm afraid I might step on one!

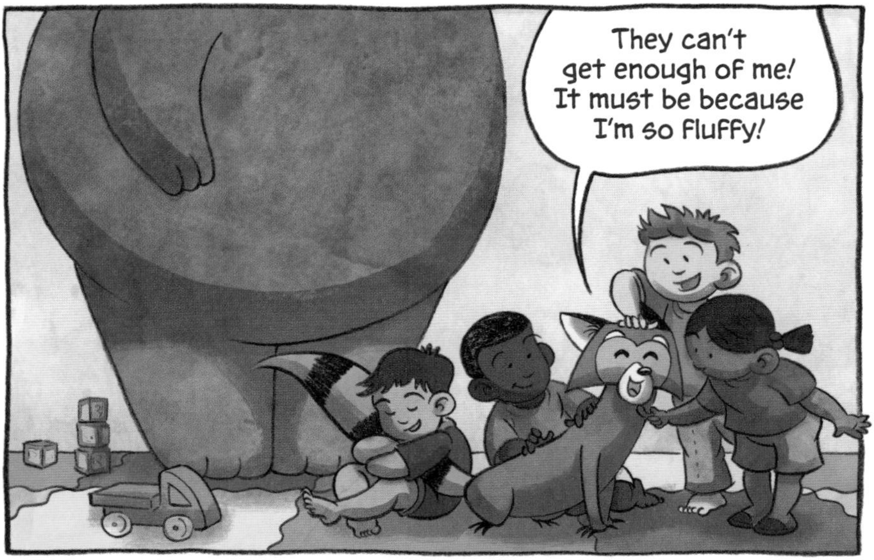
They can't get enough of me! It must be because I'm so fluffy!

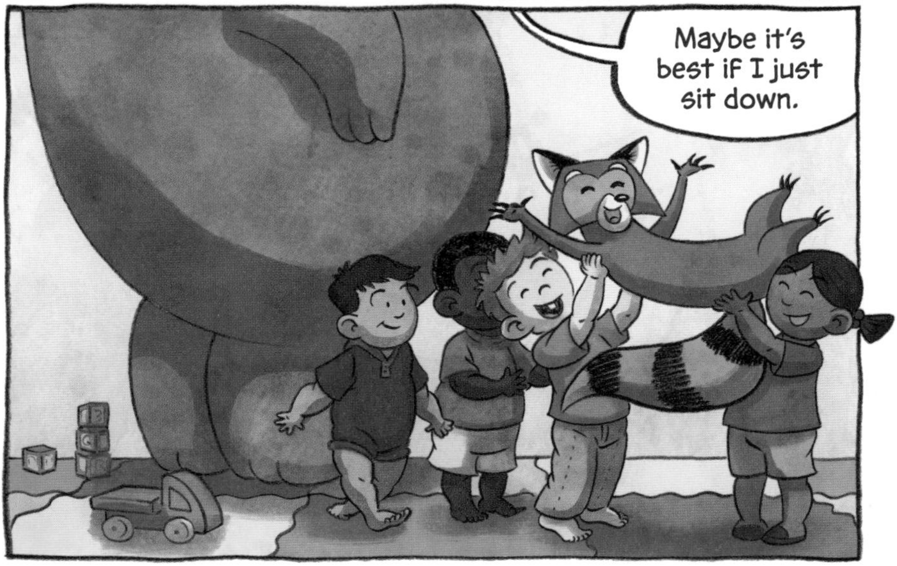
Maybe it's best if I just sit down.

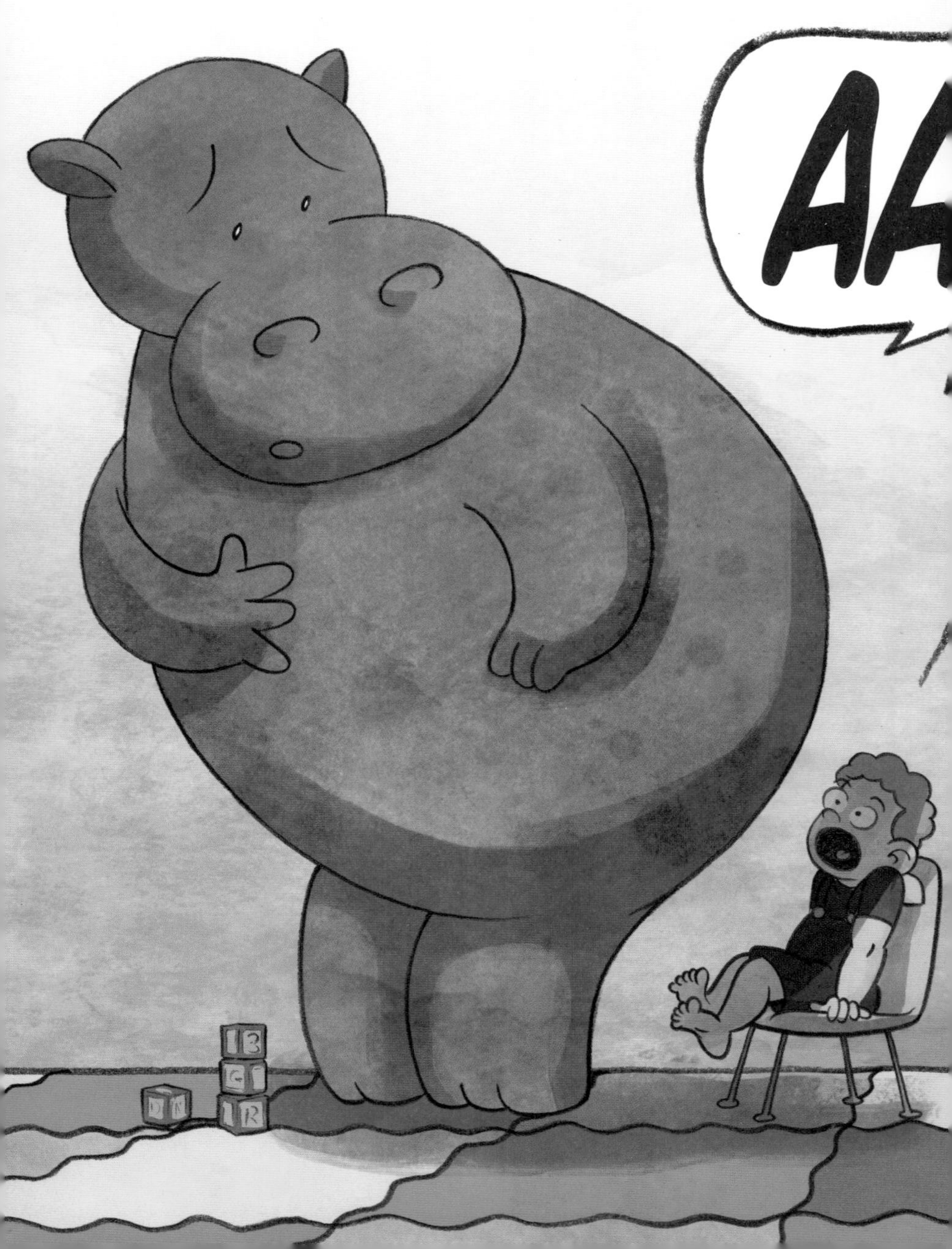
AA

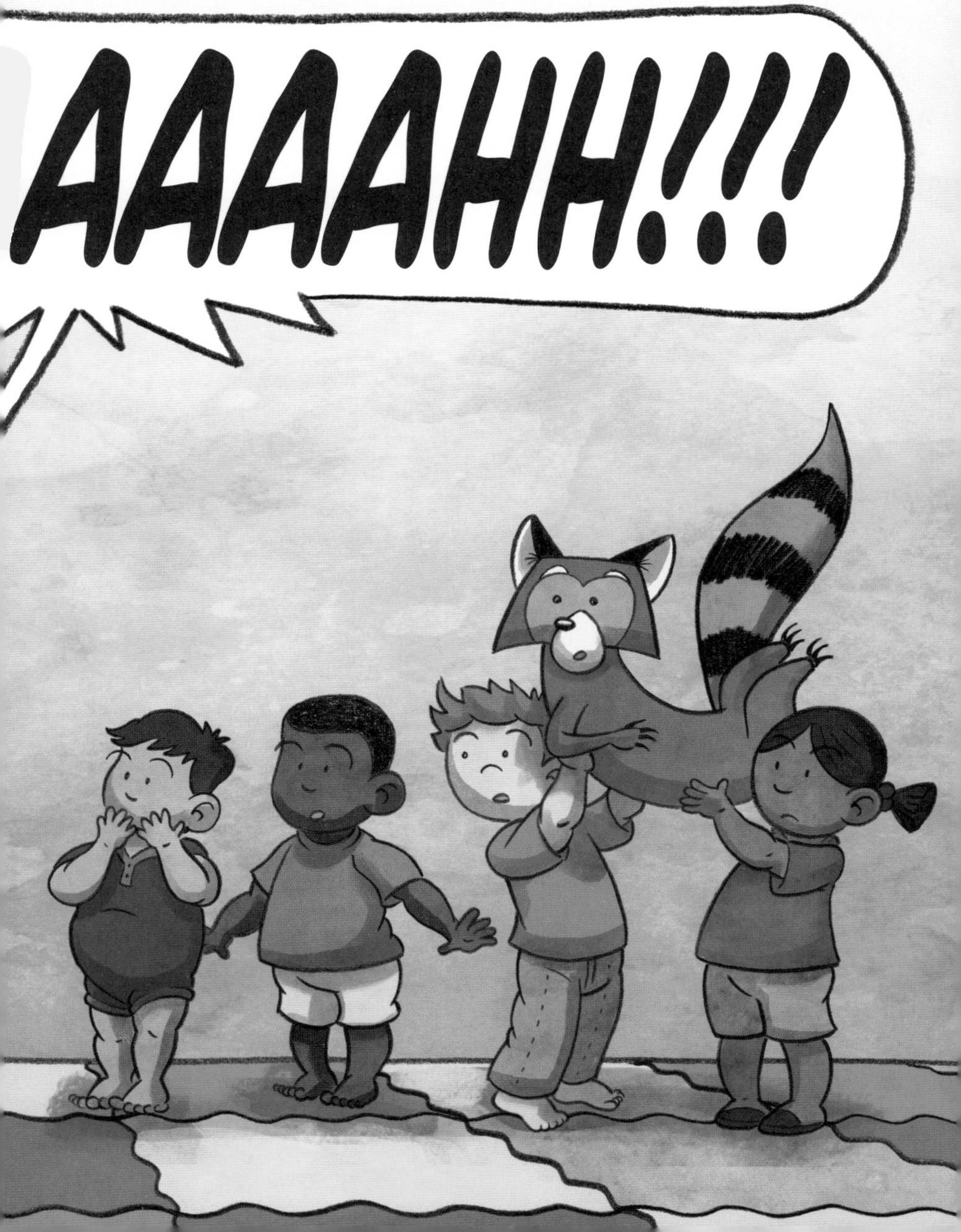
AAAAHH!!!

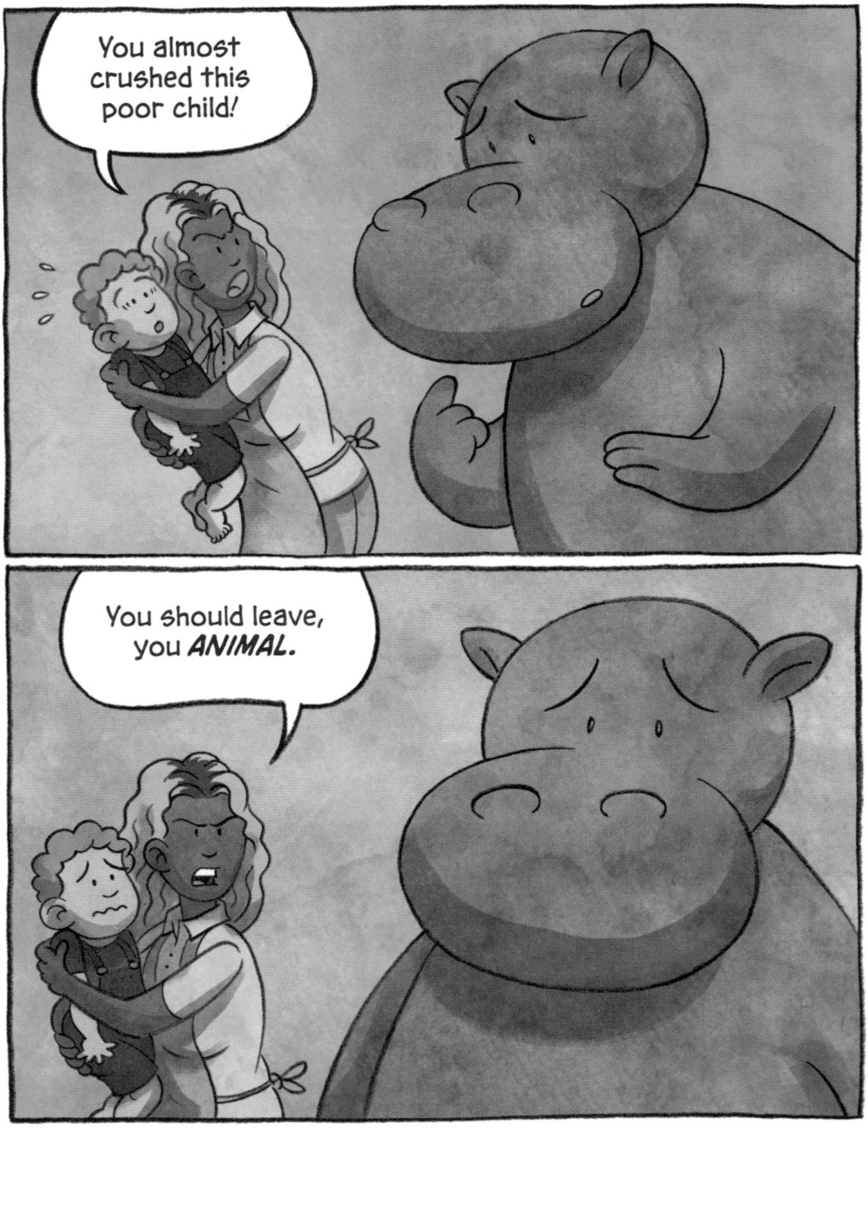
You almost crushed this poor child!
You should leave, you ***ANIMAL.***

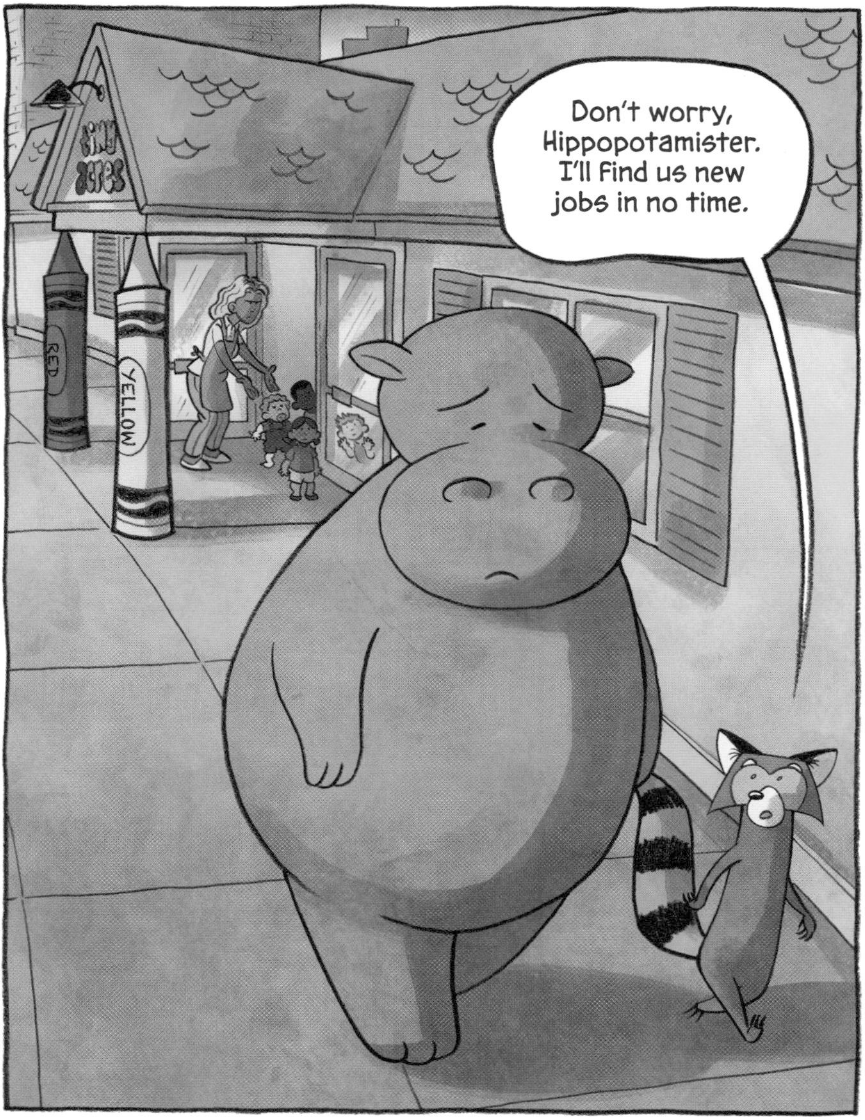
tiny acres
RED
YELLOW
Don't worry, Hippopotamister. I'll find us new jobs in no time.

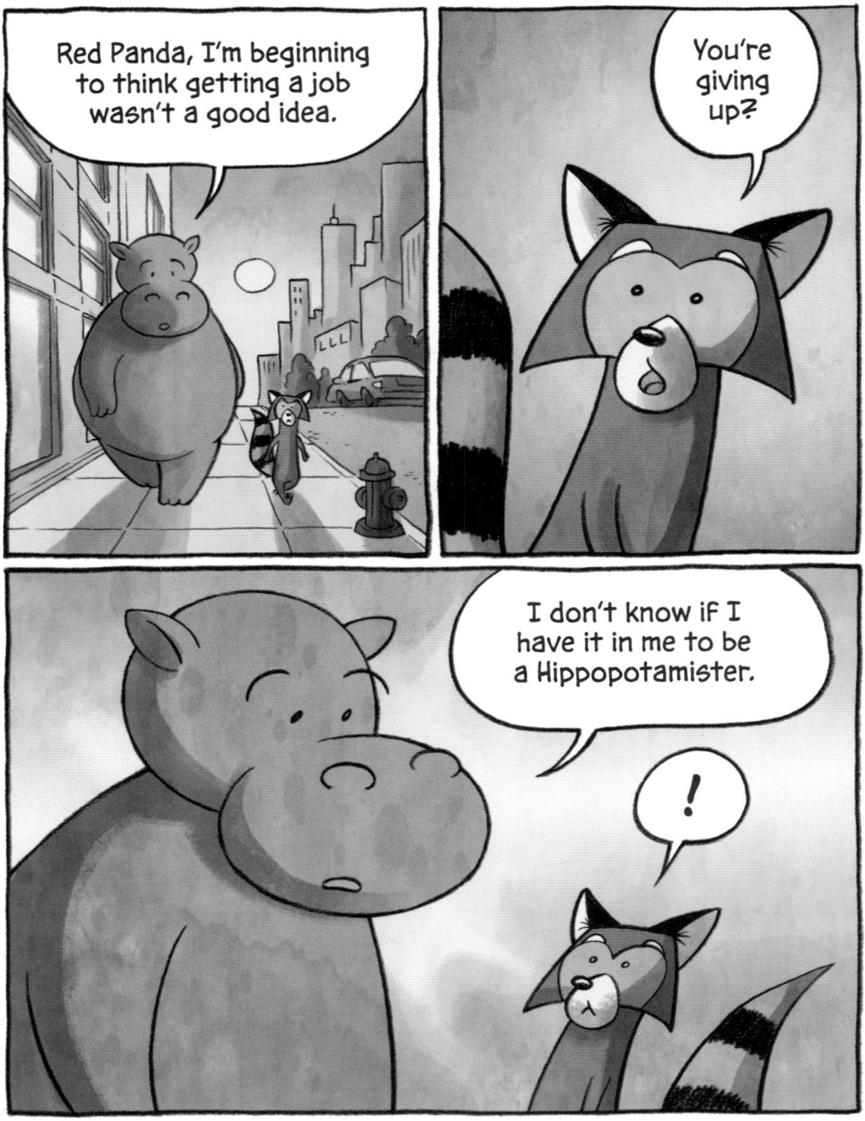
Red Panda, I'm beginning to think getting a job wasn't a good idea.
You're giving up?
I don't know if I have it in me to be a Hippopotamister.
!

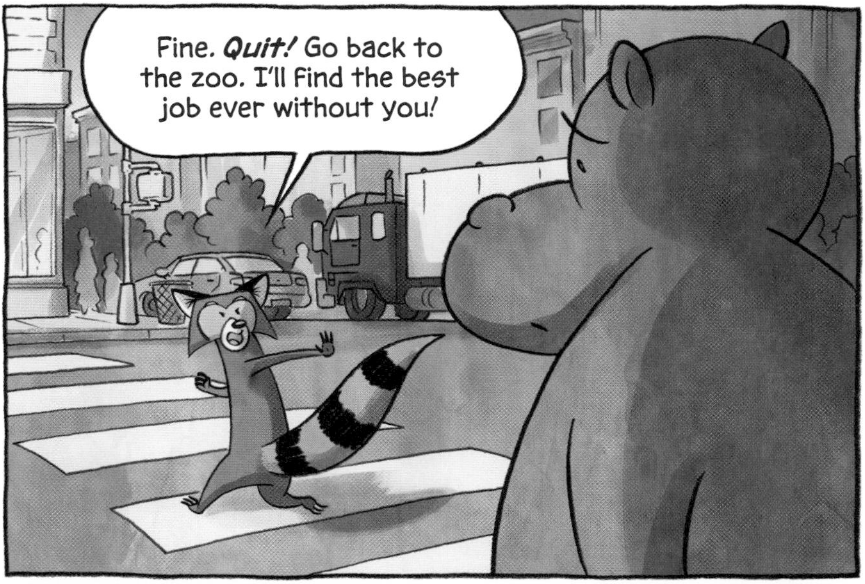
Fine. ***Quit!*** Go back to the zoo. I'll find the best job ever without you!

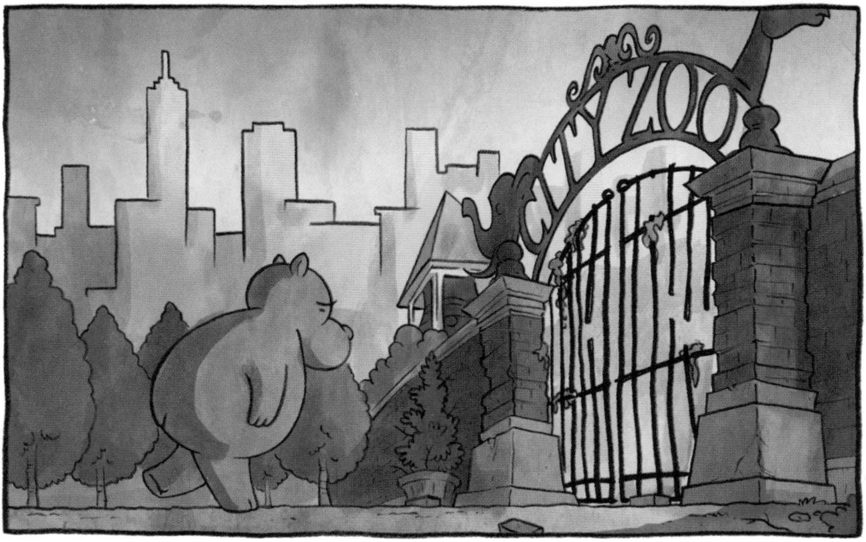
CITY ZOO

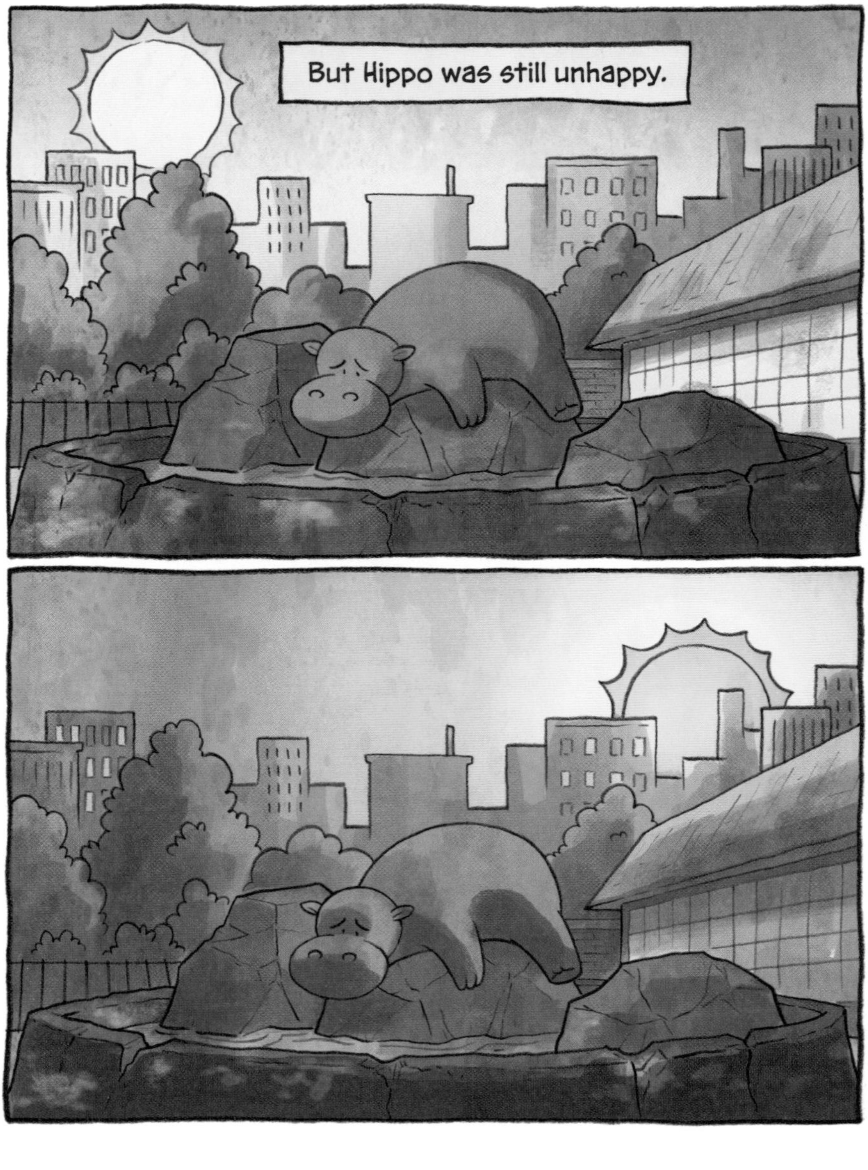
But Hippo was still unhappy.

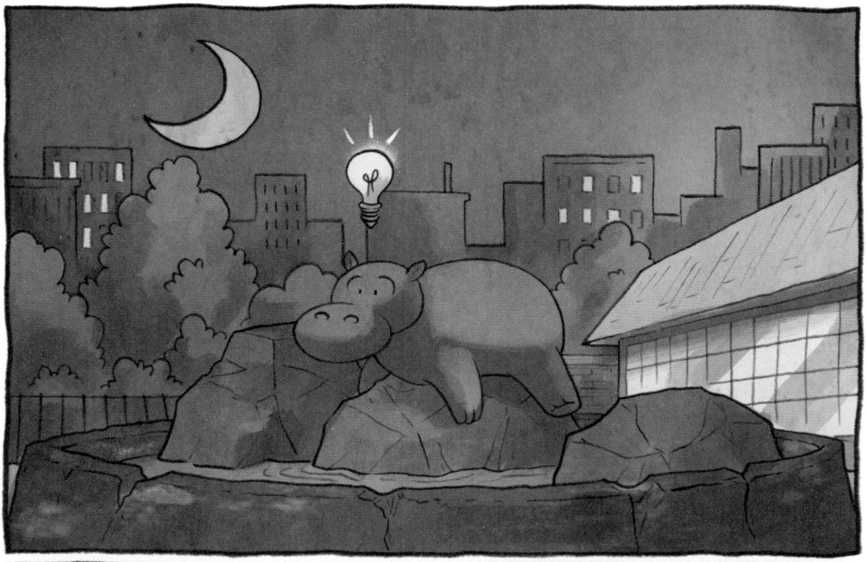

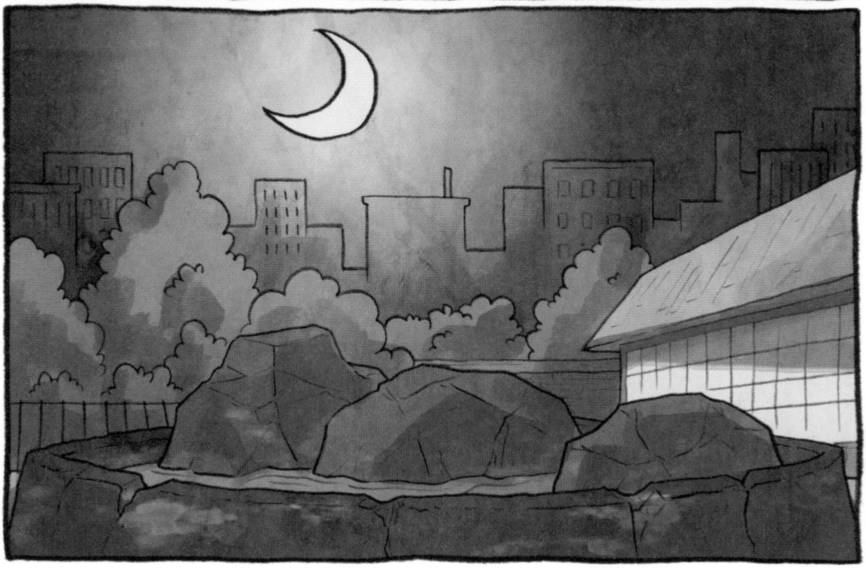

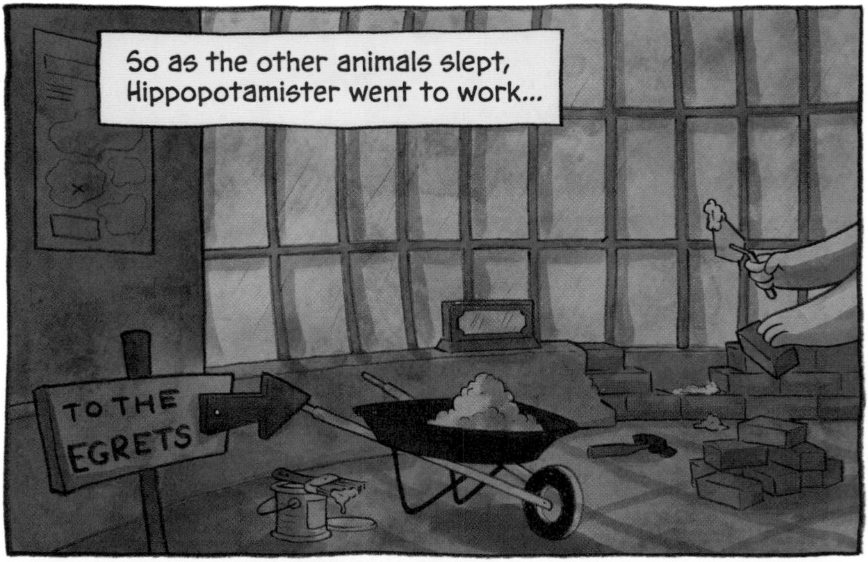
So as the other animals slept, Hippopotamister went to work...
TO THE EGRETS

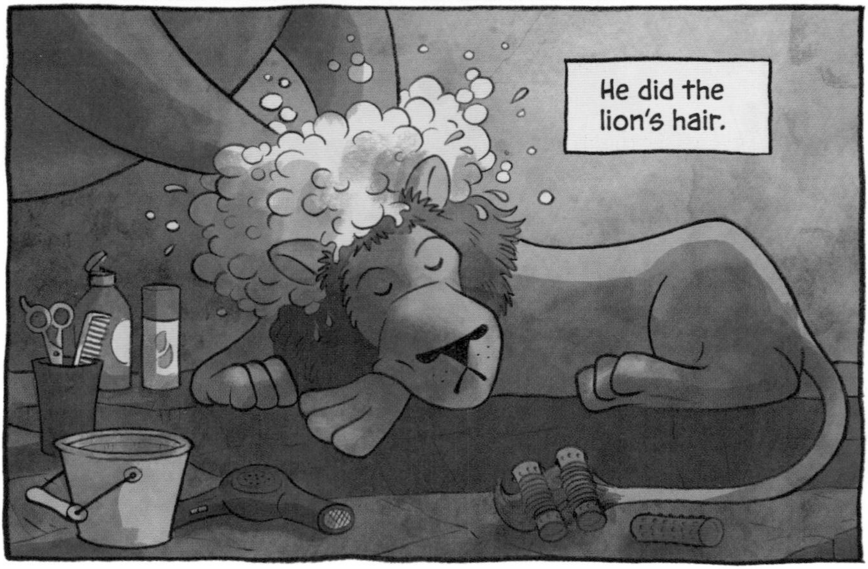
He did the lion's hair.

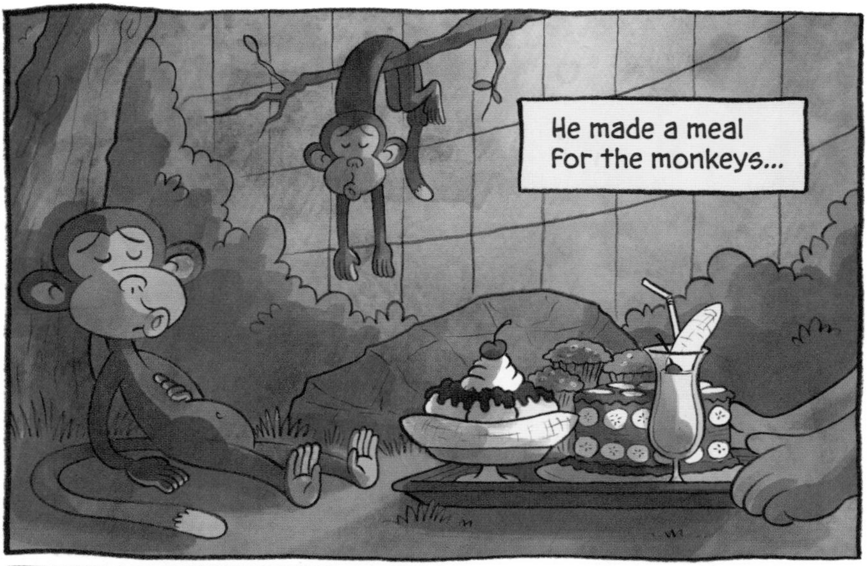
He made a meal
for the monkeys...

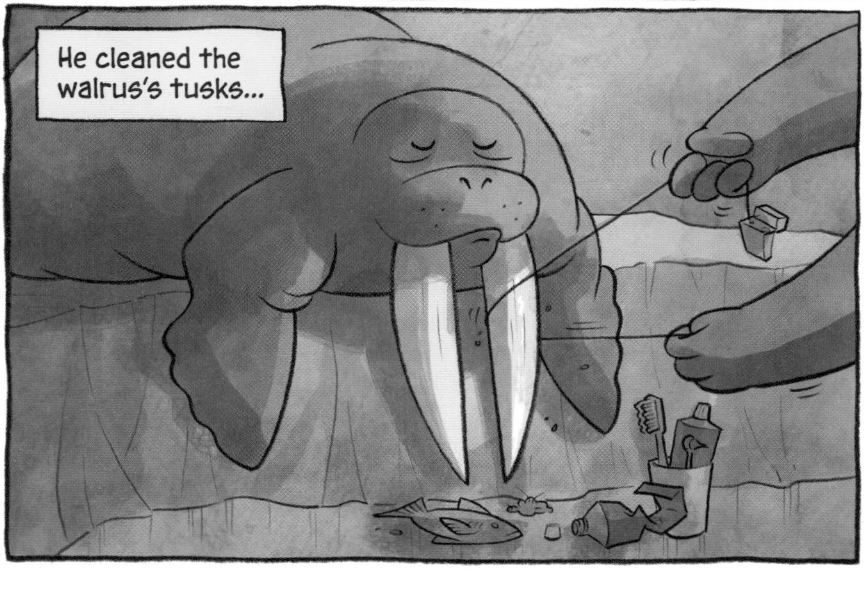
He cleaned the
walrus's tusks...

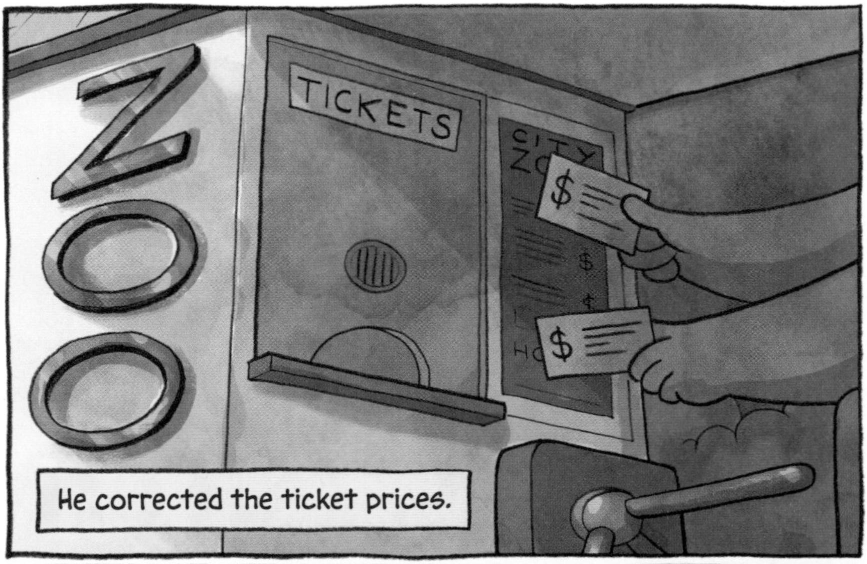
ZOO
TICKETS
CITY ZOO
He corrected the ticket prices.

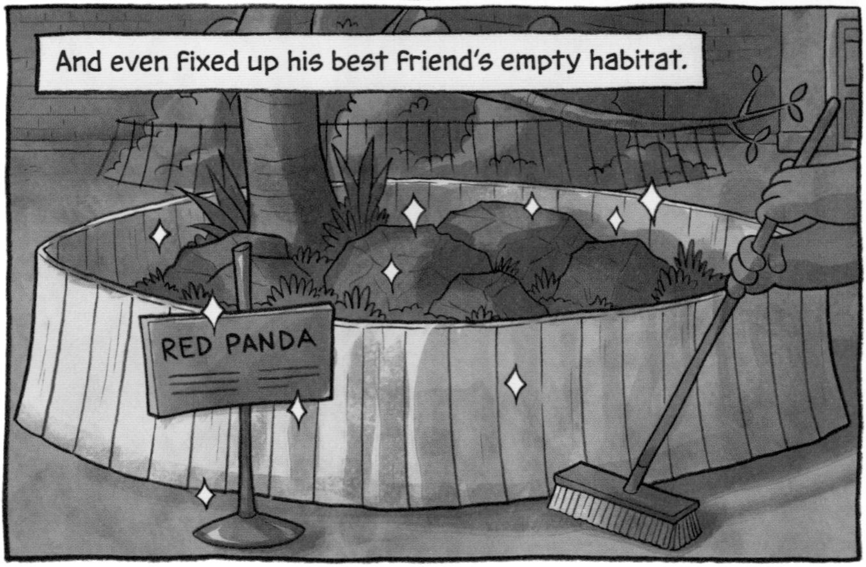
And even fixed up his best friend's empty habitat.
RED PANDA

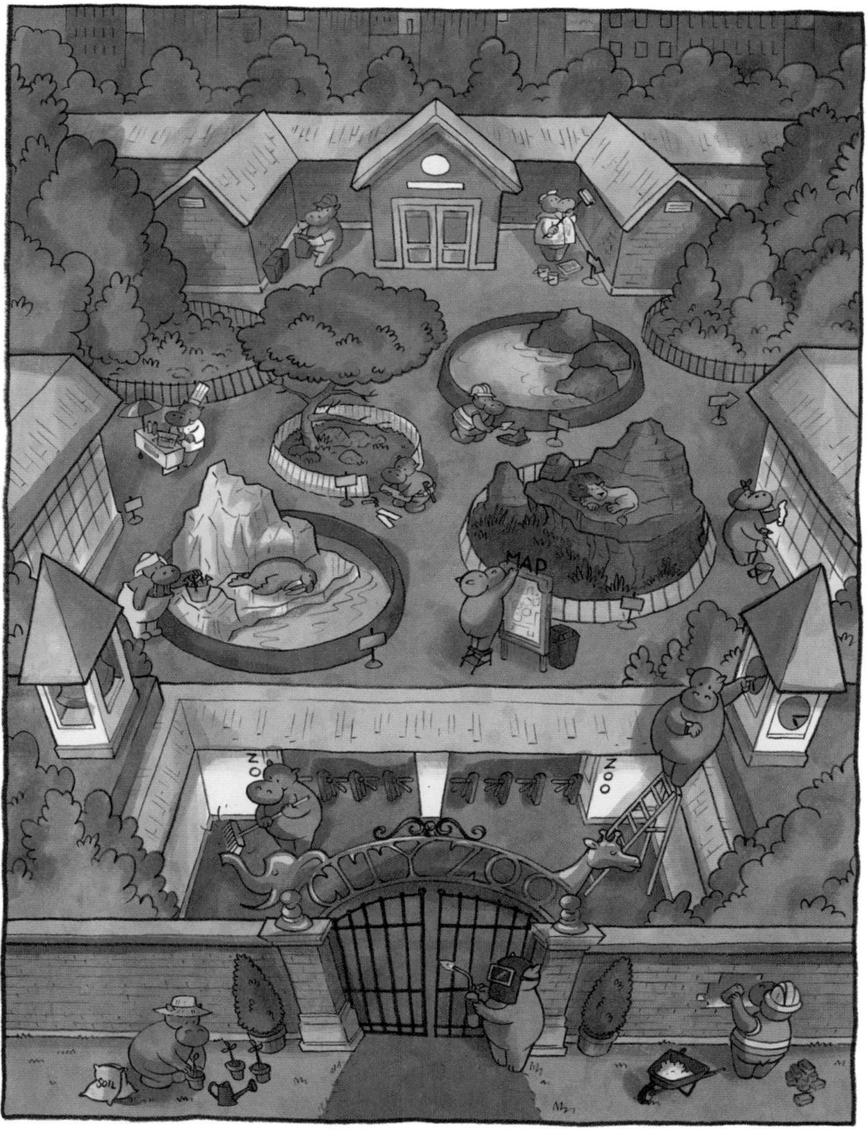
MAP
ZOO
ZOO
SOIL

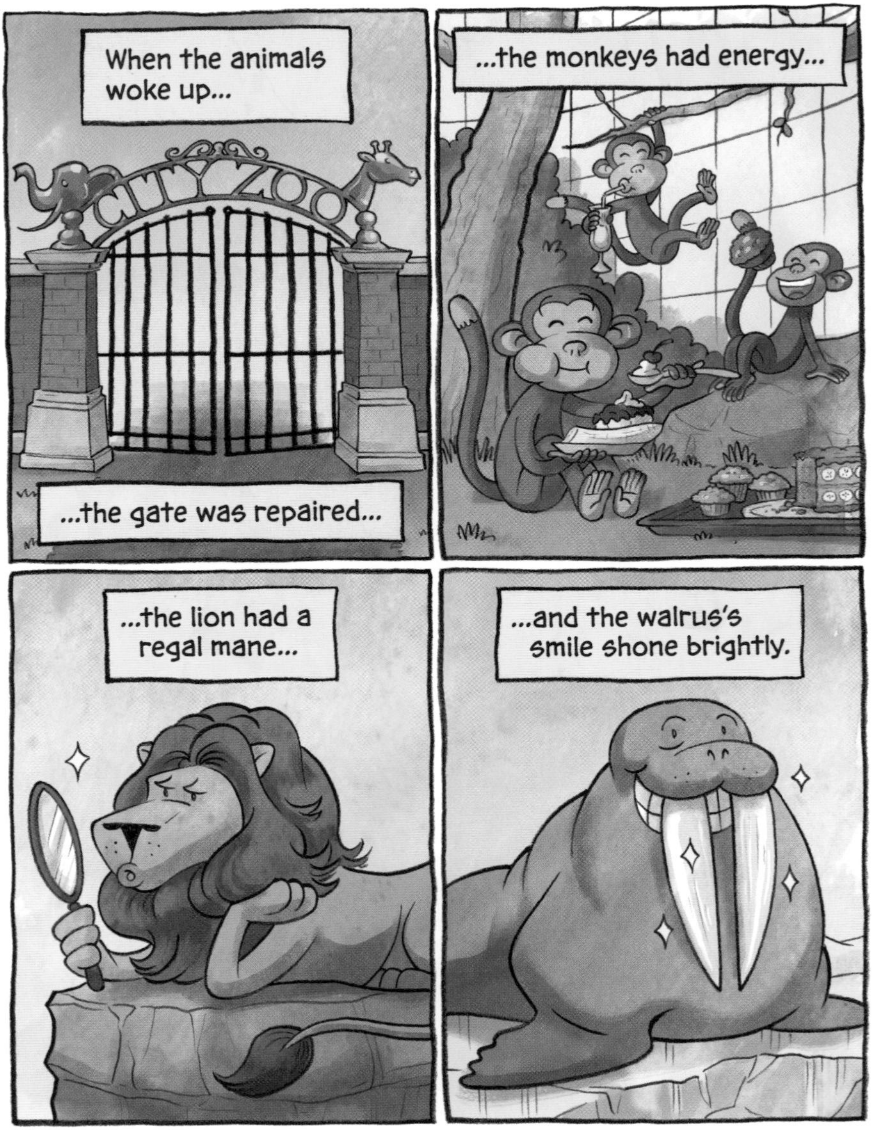
When the animals woke up...
CITY ZOO
...the gate was repaired...
...the monkeys had energy...
...the lion had a regal mane...
...and the walrus's smile shone brightly.

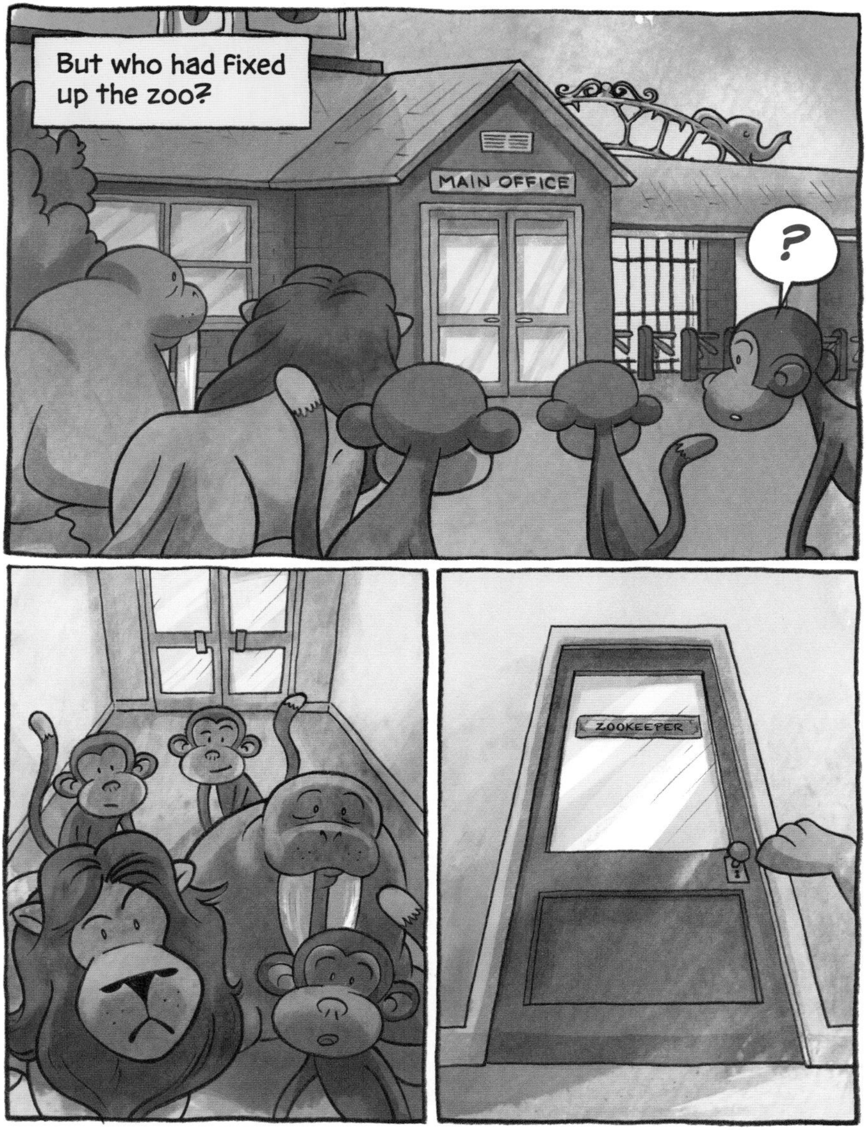
But who had fixed up the zoo?
MAIN OFFICE
?
ZOOKEEPER

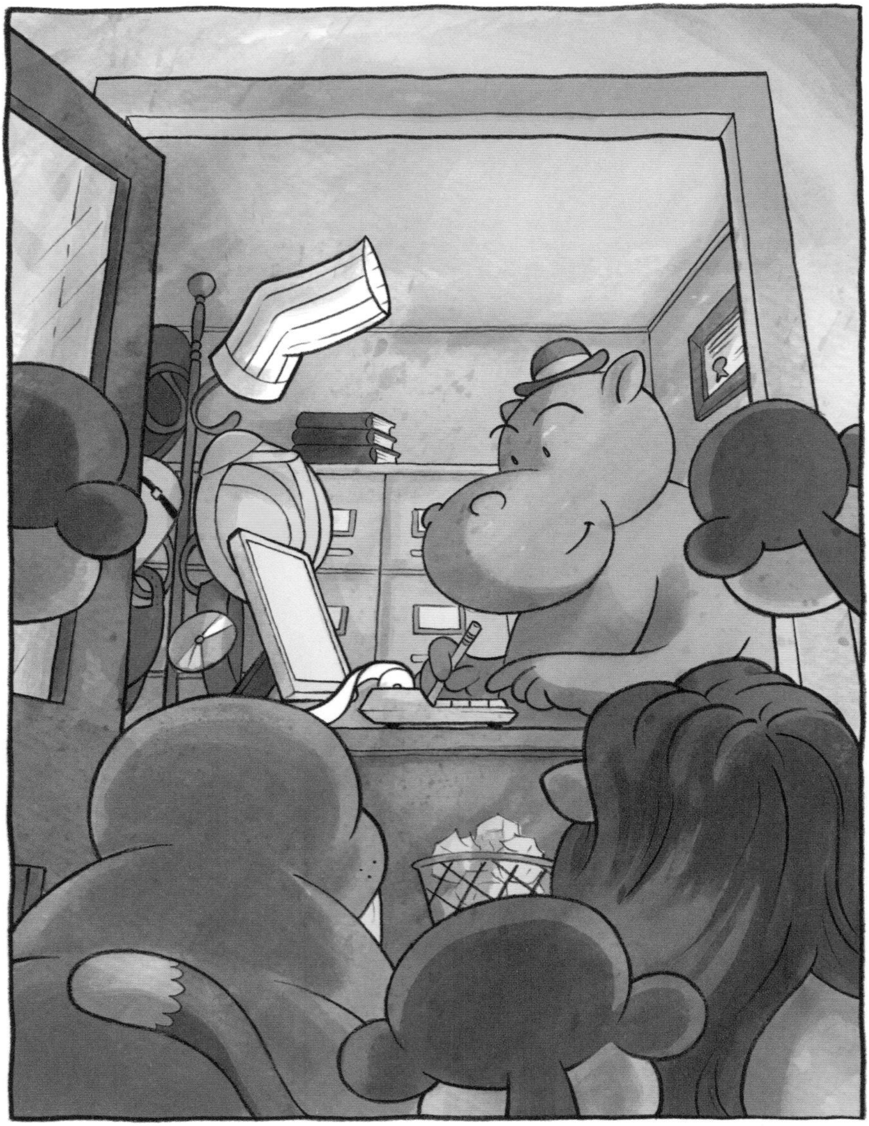

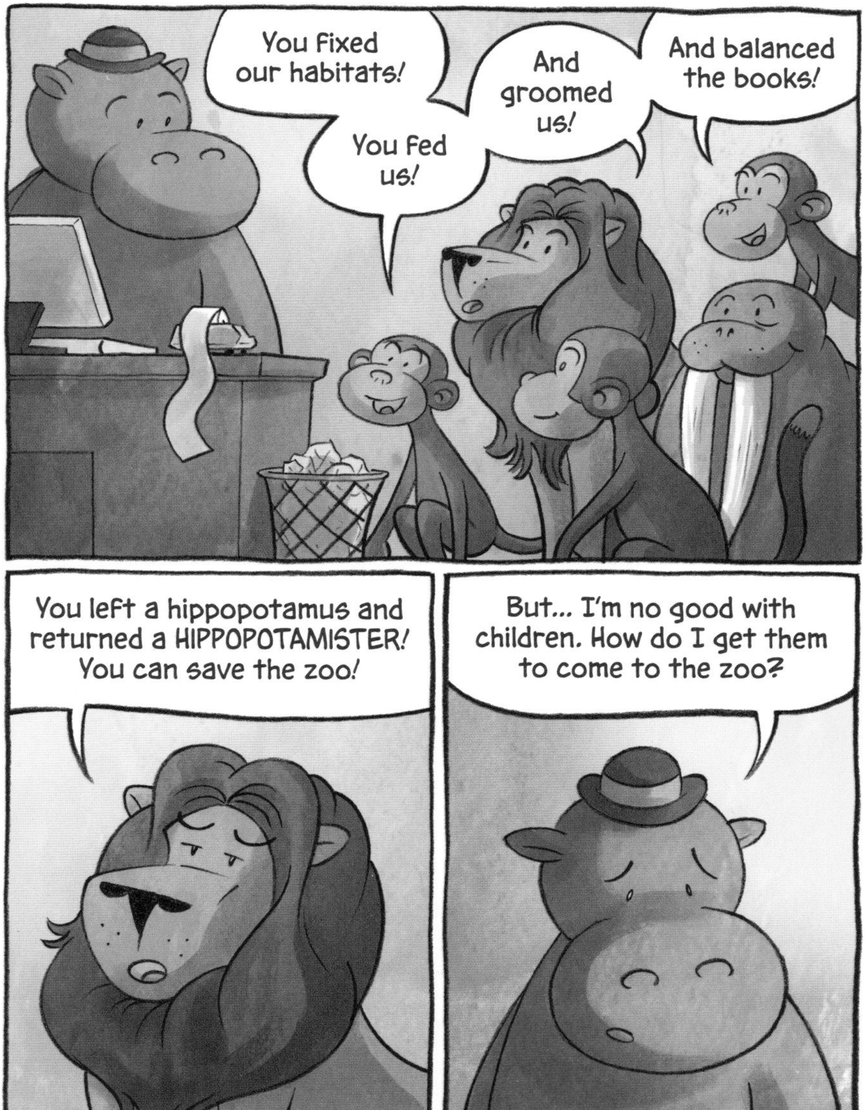
You fixed our habitats!
You fed us!
And groomed us!
And balanced the books!
You left a hippopotamus and returned a HIPPOPOTAMISTER! You can save the zoo!
But... I'm no good with children. How do I get them to come to the zoo?

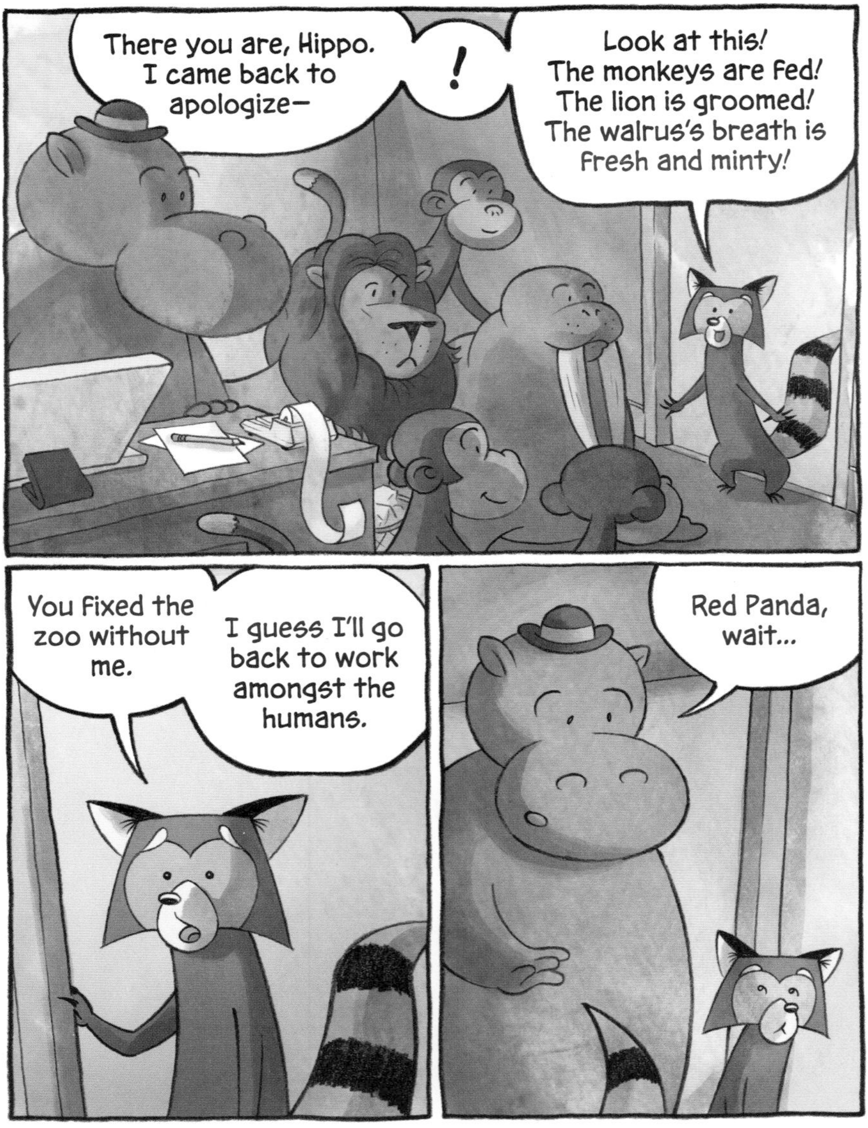
There you are, Hippo. I came back to apologize—
!
Look at this! The monkeys are fed! The lion is groomed! The walrus's breath is fresh and minty!
You fixed the zoo without me.
I guess I'll go back to work amongst the humans.
Red Panda, wait...

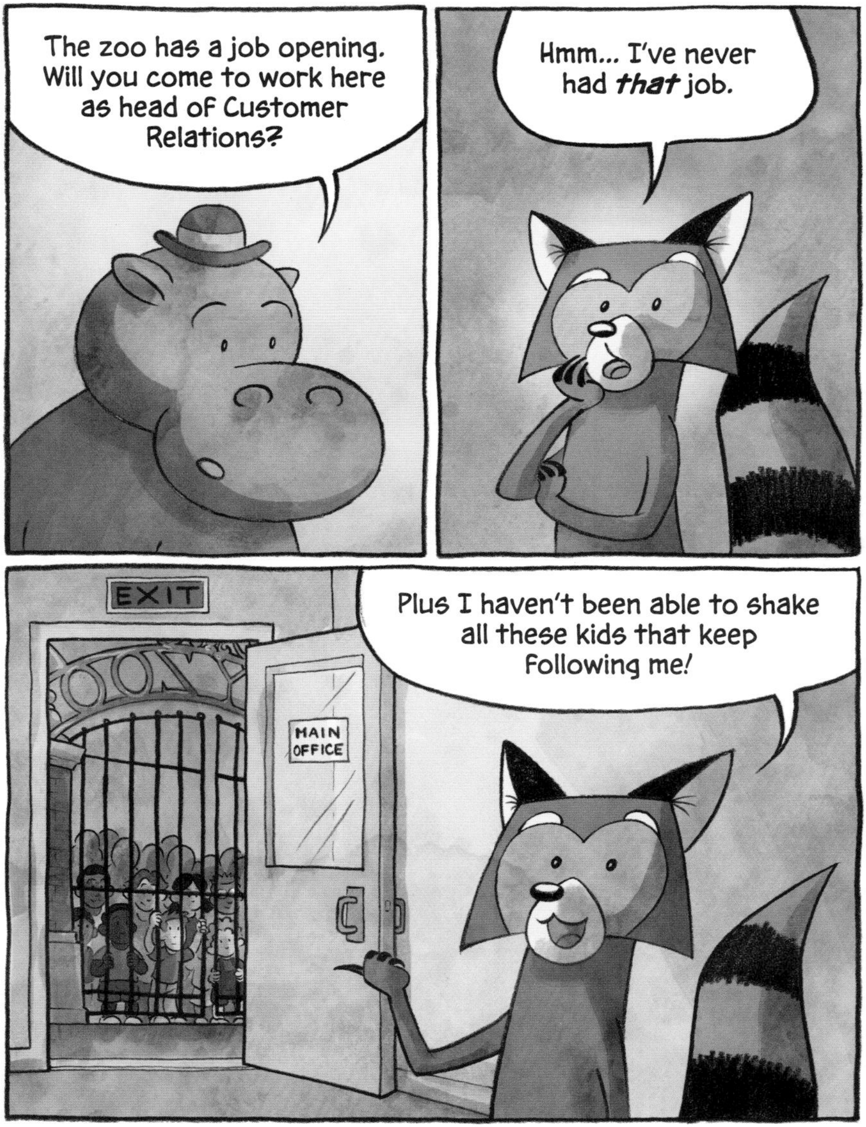
The zoo has a job opening. Will you come to work here as head of Customer Relations?
Hmm... I've never had *that* job.
EXIT
MAIN OFFICE
Plus I haven't been able to shake all these kids that keep following me!

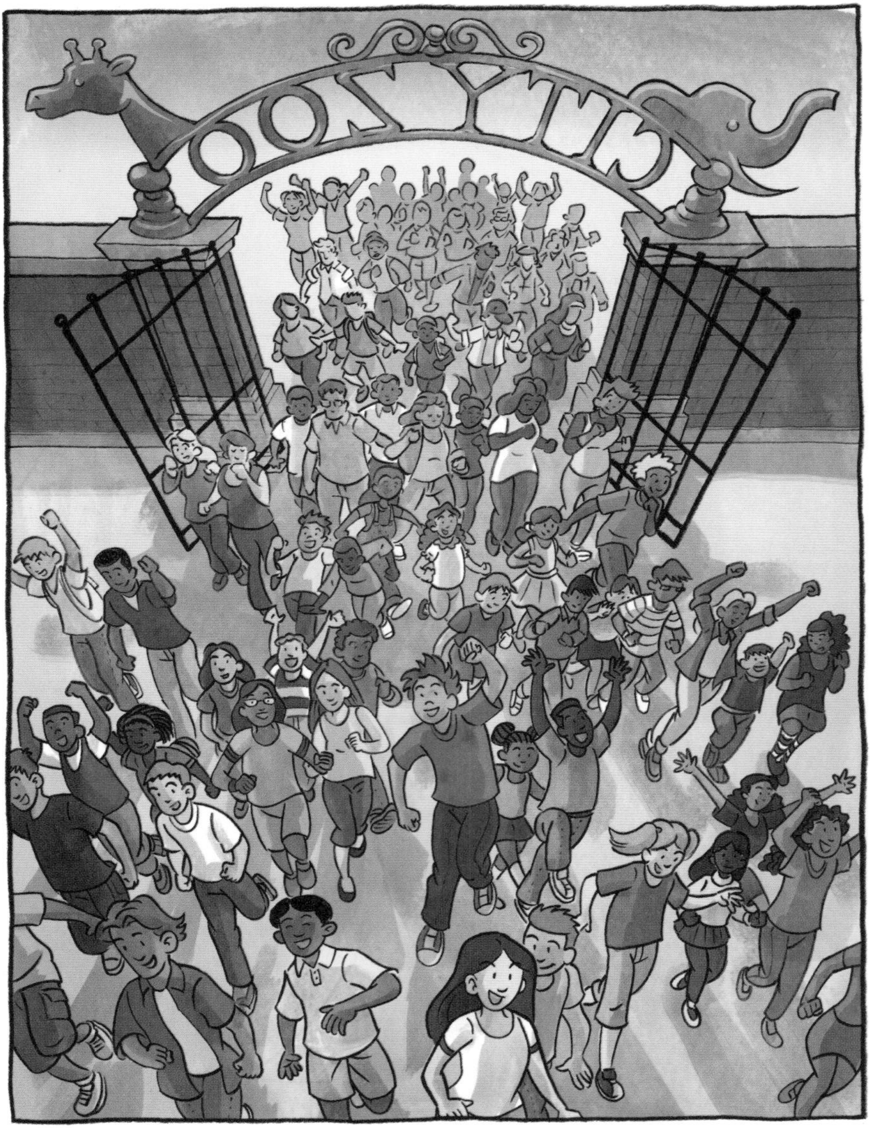

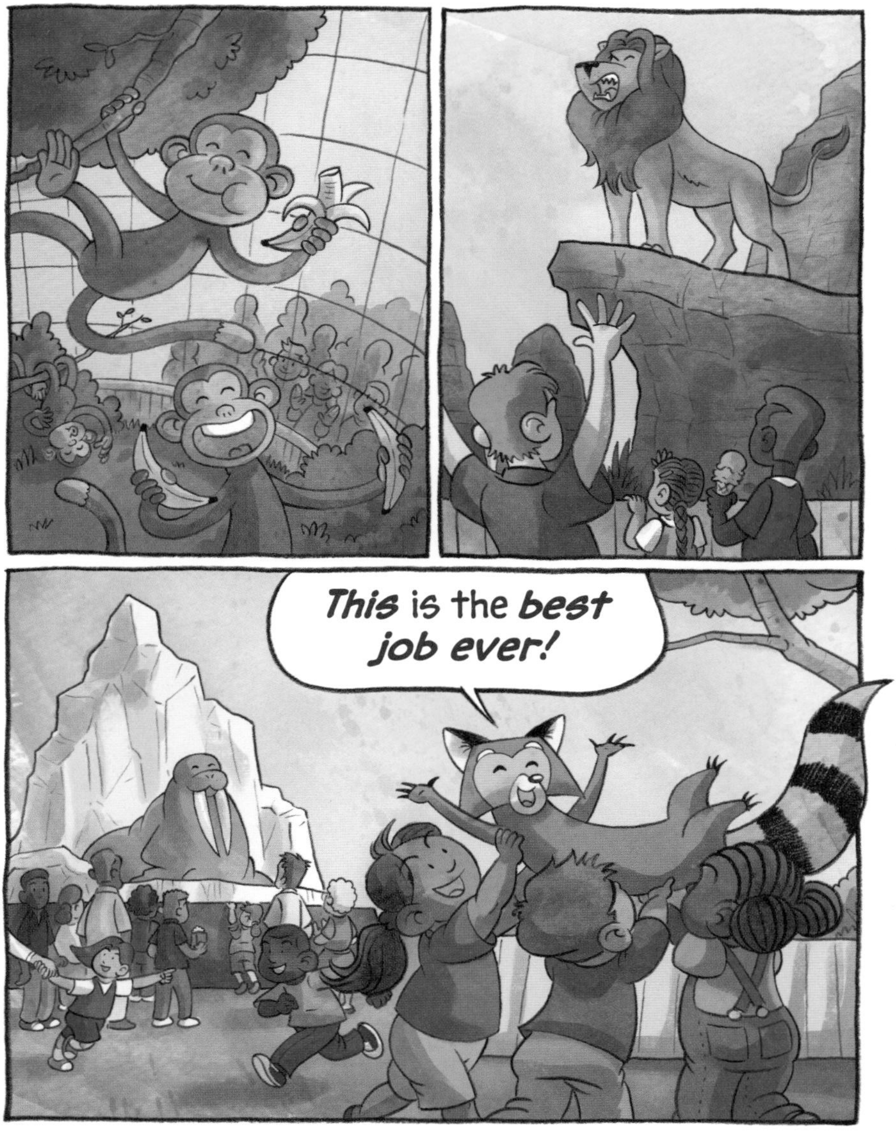
This is the *best* job ever!

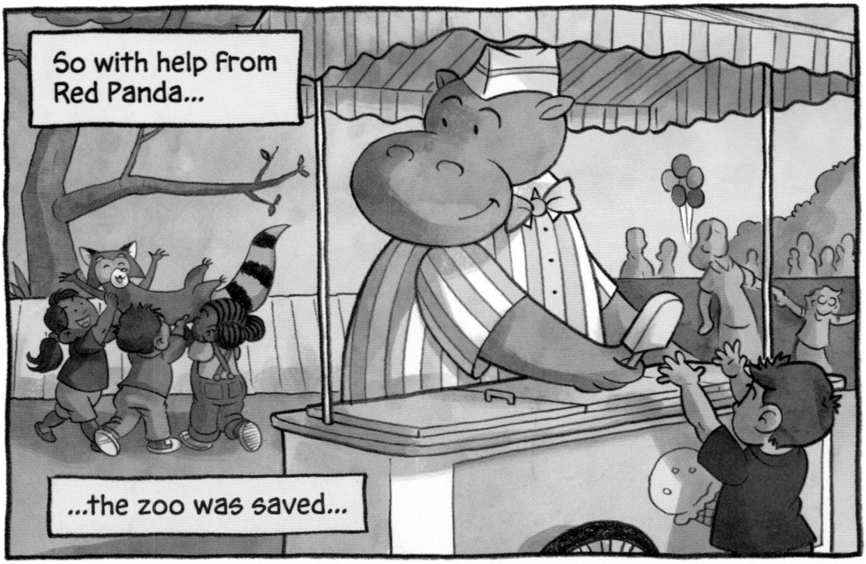
So with help from Red Panda...
...the zoo was saved...

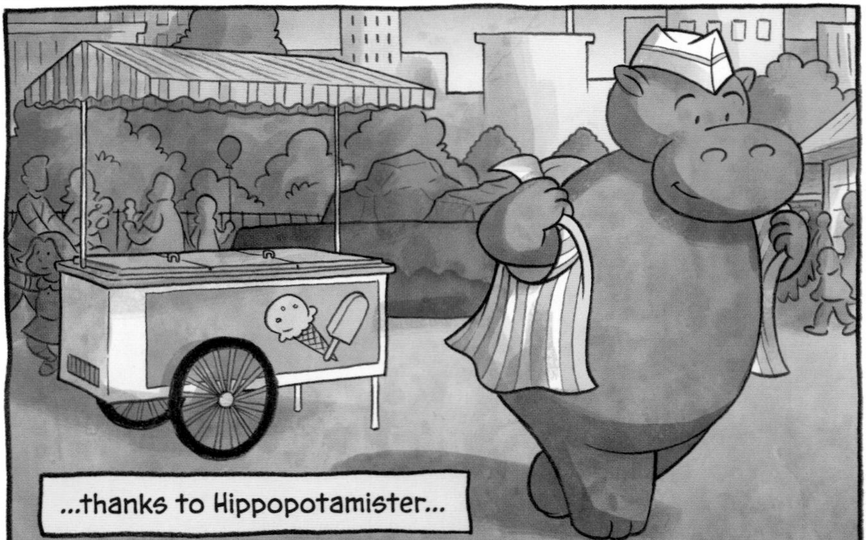
...thanks to Hippopotamister...

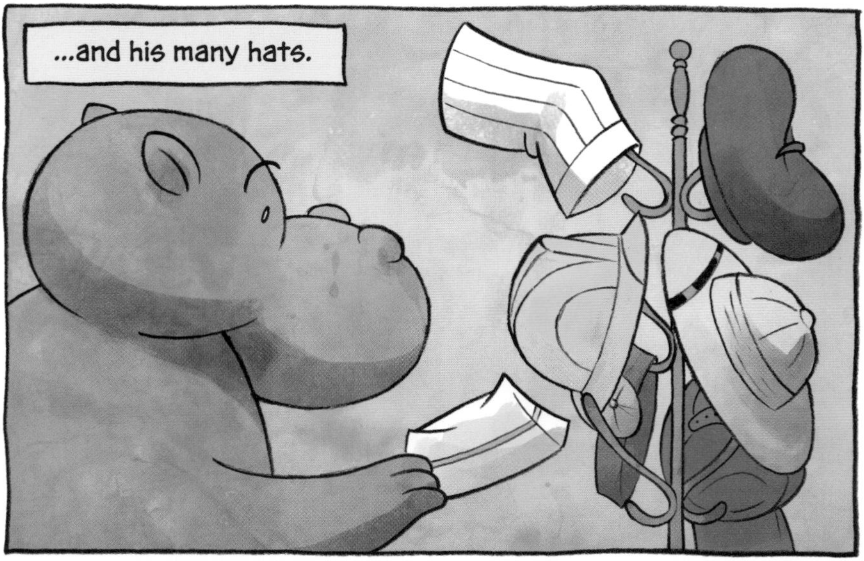
...and his many hats.

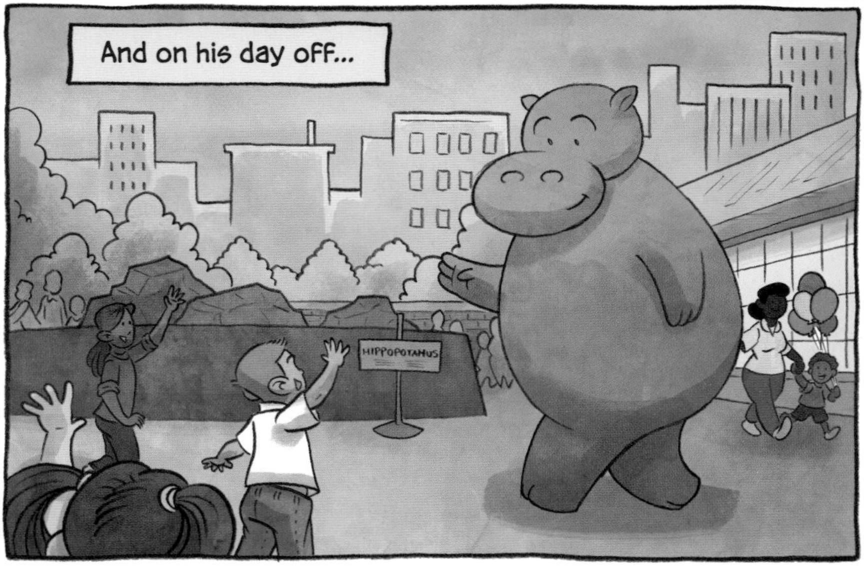
And on his day off...
HIPPOPOTAMUS

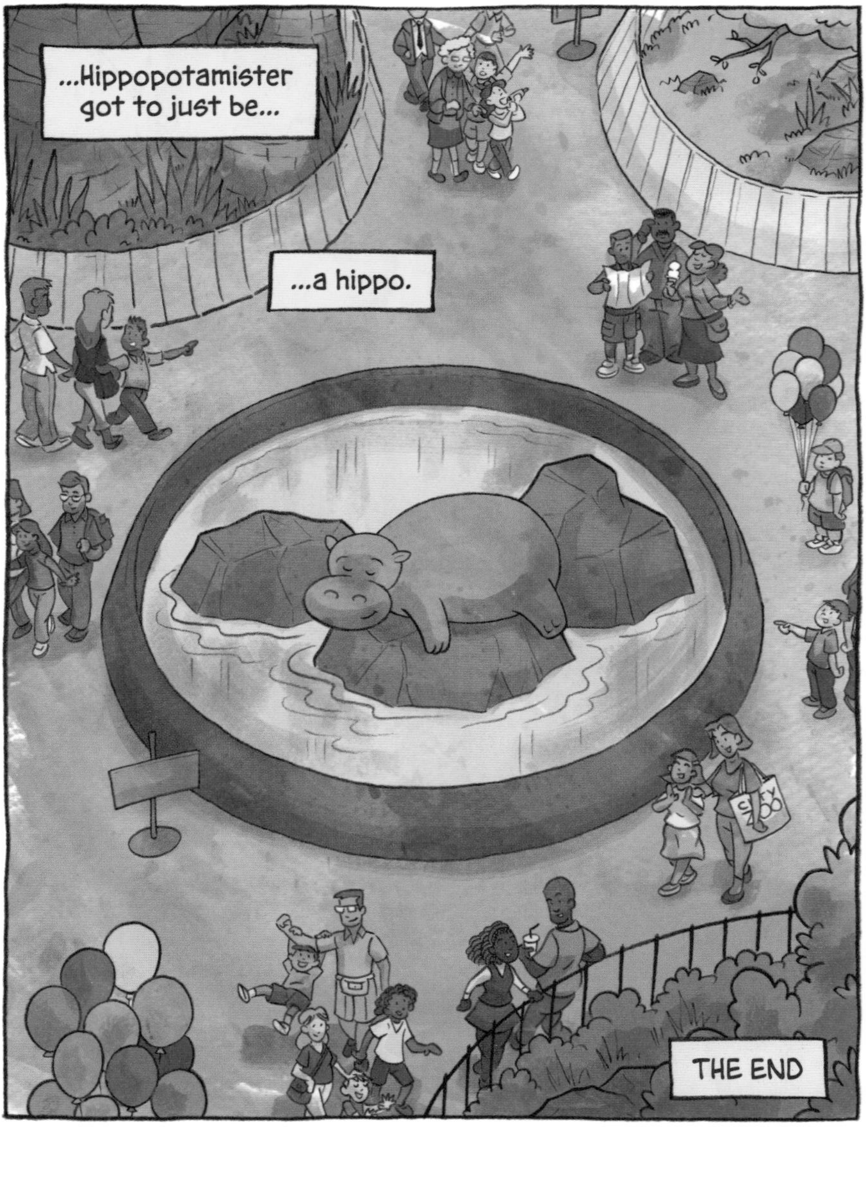
...Hippopotamister got to just be...
...a hippo.
THE END

How to draw HIPPOPOTAMISTER

1) Start with a circle, high up where his head should be.

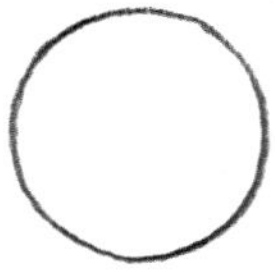

2) Draw an oval slightly overlapping the circle, for his snout.

3) Draw a large egg shape for his body.

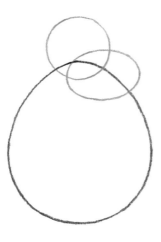

4) Add a trapezoid (a rectangle with angled sides) at the bottom for his legs.

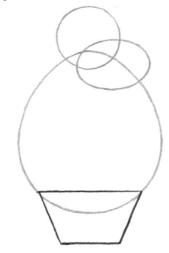

5) Draw details like his ears, eyes, nostrils, arms, and toes.

6) Erase any unwanted lines.

Finally, give Hippopotamister a hat. He's got a lot to choose from!

How to draw RED PANDA

1) Start with a trapezoid for his head. Draw lightly because Red Panda needs more erasing than Hippopotamister.

2) Draw a long tube shape for his body, almost like a hot dog.

3) Add a small egg shape for his snout, and triangles for his ears.

4) His arms, legs, and tail are more complex shapes and might take practice.

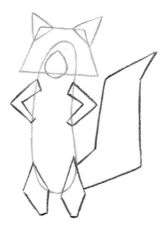

5) Draw details like his ears, eyes, mouth, fingers, toes, and tail stripes.

6) Fill in his ears and tail stripes and erase any unwanted lines.

Red Panda likes hats, too. Don't forget to add his best friend, Hippo!

Read the John Patrick Green Collection!

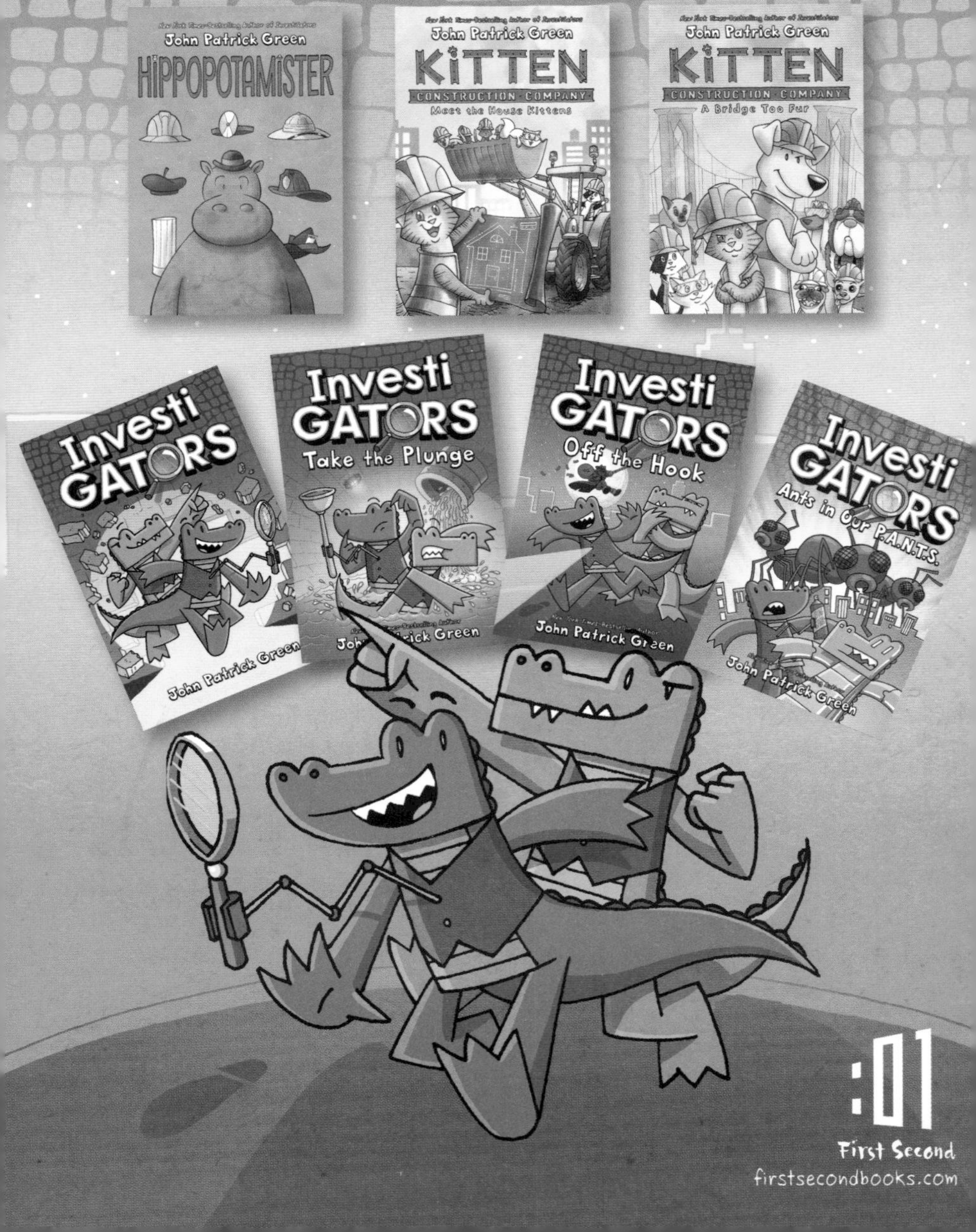
John Patrick Green
HIPPOPOTAMISTER
John Patrick Green
KITTEN
CONSTRUCTION COMPANY
Meet the House Kittens
John Patrick Green
KITTEN
CONSTRUCTION COMPANY
A Bridge Too Fur
InvestiGATORS
John Patrick Green
InvestiGATORS
Take the Plunge
InvestiGATORS
Off the Hook
John Patrick Green
InvestiGATORS
Ants in Our P.A.N.T.S.
John Patrick Green

First Second
firstsecondbooks.com